THE
DAY
Stand

SHAYLA HART

D1566728

The 7 Day Stand

SHAYLA HART

Copyright

Dedications

To all my smut loving Kings & Queens
This ones for you

"IN THE MATTER OF LOVE, AGE IS NOTHING BUT A NUMBER."
-SHAYLA HART

Playlist

AIRPLANE - MAX OAZO, MOONESSA
HAPPIER THAN EVER - KELLY CLARKSON
I HATE MYSELF FOR LOVING YOU - JOAN JETT & THE
BLACK HEARTS
SAME PLACE - JOY
WHISPER - ABLE HEART
SWEAT - ZAYN
MIDDLE OF THE NIGHT - ELLEY DUHE
OKAY - CHASE ATLANTIC
WILDFIRE - NATE SMITH
UNDER THE INFLUENCE - CHRIS BROWN
WAY DOWN WE GO - KALEO
BACKSEAT - DANIEL DI ANGELO
NEVER TEAR US APART - BISHOP BRIGGS
ITS ALL OVER - ADAM SKINNER & DAN SKINNER, DAVE
JAMES..
STAY WITH ME- SAM SMITH
MY ALL - LARISSA LAMBERT

FULL PLAYLIST ON SPOTIFY..

Pssst, wait a minute...

If you're a lover of books with a plot, reading this novella may leave you a little unsatisfied, simply because it is written with no plot or storyline in mind.

This book was written for those who crave smut or are in need of a quick steamy read before jumping into something a little more heavy— just as I am about to with my next book.

However, if you choose to read on, this is your warning—don't say I didn't warn you, though I truly hope you enjoy anyway! :-)

Happy reading, Love!

Love always,

Shayla Hart

Chapter 1
Savi

Airplane - Max Oazo, Moonessa

PROLOGUE

OH, I effed up.

I effed up grandly and I am not the least bit sorry about it. Nope, not a single fuck in sight even as I'm sprawled out on top of the imposingly heavy and ornate solid oak desk with my bare ass hanging off and my knees by my ears, while the unlawfully handsome silver fox laps skillfully and appreciatively at my pussy.

"Jesus, Logan. Fuck, don't stop." I whimper urgently, reaching up over my head to clutch at the edge of the desk with a deathly grip as he slowly but torturously drives me to the apex of that bittersweet release with every languid stroke of his wicked tongue on my pulsing clit.

Liquid grey eyes lift and lock with mine. The mischief and desire that gleams in his eyes sends a delicious shiver cascading down the length of my spine. Holy shit, I'm in way over my head with this man, but for the very life of me, I can't seem to get enough of him, that mouth, or that mammoth pierced cock of his.

Yes, *pierced.*

This is so out of character for me. I've never been one to have a crush on an older man, especially one that is twice my age, and definitely not my ex-boyfriend's dad. I mean, unless you count the celebrity hotties. You know the ones, George Clooney, Richard Gere and Daniel Craig, Oh, Alec Baldwin. Boy , I spent a good chunk of my teenage years obsessing over Daniel Craig. He's still such a dish and I wouldn't think twice nor have any shame about dropping my panties for him.

Though, they don't hold a candle to the beauteous Logan *effing* Pierce. No exaggeration, the man is built like a mountain of muscles, a gorgeous face I'm sure is carved by archangels, and don't get me started on those deep commanding grey eyes that not only stifles your breath, but also make you involuntarily want to hit your knees in front of him.

My ex-boyfriend Trent clearly snatched up his father's good looks, but none of his characteristics. Hard to believe he fathered such a callous prick. The boy is a bona fide asshole, but for some reason that seems to be my type. I always attract the worst type of men. The rotten parasites that love to suck the life right out of you and drop you on your ass like you're nothing more than a worthless sack of cow dung.

Despite mine and Trent's rocky relationship and having my heart broken by him countless times over and over I never learn and still let him worm his way back to me. Every time believing that he will change.

Why? Because I love him. At least, I thought I did, and I considered him to be—at that time—the best sex I ever had... until his dad.

Yes, I'm fully aware that my morals are disreputable, however it's hard to scrape together a single a fuck when he devours pussy like it's his last supper and my pussy is his holy grail. Who am I to deny him as well as myself the pleasure?

Want to know the most screwed up part of it all? My ex-boyfriend— his *son*—and his ex-wife are somewhere in the house and could bust in at any moment and catch us. The imminent threat of us getting caught at any given moment only adds to the thrill and heightens my pleasure. My pussy has never ached so raveningly nor ever before craved a man so desperately as I do him.

In the handful of days I've known him, Logan Pierce has without a doubt ruined me for all other men.

Liquid heat rushes through my body rapidly and coils deep in my belly as I grind myself against his mouth, chasing my orgasm. "Oh yes, yes, I'm coming." I bite down on my lower lip hard to quieten the whimper about to escape me when Logan lands a hard slap on my left butt cheek and squeezes the flesh firmly. Damn, that's going to leave a nice bruise. I suppose I deserved that for riling him up earlier.

A low throaty growl emits from Logan and thrums right through me when my pussy pulses as I fall over the edge and surrender to the blinding pleasure that wreaks havoc over my body one enchanting wave at a time.

"Logan..." I moan curling my fingers in his hair and grip tight till I ride out every last ripple of pleasure that he's bestowing me with, whilst greedily drinking up every drop of my girl cum. "Shit." I pant, smiling lazily when he kisses the spot he slapped before.

"I'll never tire of watching you cum for me, sweetheart." Logan burrs lifting me upright so he could brush a kiss over my lips. I, of course, readily welcome the kiss, parting my lips for him to get a secondhand taste of myself on his tongue. Mm, there's something so erotic about having my taste linger on his lips while he's walking around conversing with the guests attending the party. A party he is hosting and the company I work for is managing, at his lavish stately home in honor of the twentieth anniversary of his company. Pierce Enterprise Holding. Twenty years ago, and fresh out of university with a bachelor's degree in business, Logan started his own company in construction. Now at forty, he's the owner of a multimillion-dollar company with offices all around the United States.

3

"Well, it's a good thing I'm rather fond of coming for you then, Mr. Pierce." Logan flashes me a sexy grin and draws my mouth to his for another ardent kiss that leaves me moaning and burning for more when he pulls back.

"You have no idea how desperately I want to carry you to my bedroom right now and spend the night fucking you savagely." He admits and licks those sinful lips.

I lower my eyes to the straining bulge in his grey trousers and smile impishly. I drag my finger teasingly over the length of his throbbing cock, and it pulses under my touch. Logan sucks in a quick breath through his teeth and rocks himself up desperate for more contact and his eyes close.

"I may have some idea."

"Savi," he growls throatily, his large hand comes up and he grips my jaw. His steely eyes gazing penetratingly into my hazel ones. "I have absolutely no reservations over taking you right here in my office. Fuck Trent, April and the hundred odd guests roaming the place. I couldn't give a rat's ass if Jesus himself descends from heaven and catches us. I will fuck you like a savage and make you scream my name so loud the dead will hear you and be envious."

I gulp, swallowing against the dryness of my throat. Fuck me, that's so hot and if I weren't so concerned about us getting caught, I'd beg for him to make good on his threat.

But we can't, because he has way too much to lose and while I find it endearing that he wants me enough to risk it, we don't really know much about one another, and I wouldn't ever forgive myself if he wound up losing his son and his reputation. I only met him four days ago for goodness' sake.

It was only supposed to be a meaningless one-night stand.

Hold on, I should probably take you back to the very beginning.

My name is Savannah West, I'm twenty-one years old and I live in San Diego, California...

Chapter 2
Savi

Happier Than Ever - Kelly Clarkson

Four days before...

"Sav, look, I really like you babe, but I'm not in a good head space right now. I need some time to focus on myself and I can't do that while I'm someone's boyfriend."

I sit there numbly staring at Trent across the table, my gaze rakes over his handsome face. His eyes, a gorgeous concoction of greenish blue, always reminds of the Indian ocean. His mousy brown hair is kept long and swept back neatly out of his face. Sort of like Leonardo Di Caprio in his younger years. God, I hate that he's so beautiful. I can't help but wonder why he chose to date me.

I swallow the painful lump forming in my throat. This jackass is dumping me... *again*, two days before my birthday. I don't know why I keep doing this to myself. I know he's never going to fully commit to me, but I still take him back. I'm such a mug for allowing myself to fall for him when it's clear he doesn't give a hot steaming crap about me. At least his excuse this time has more validity than the last time he broke up with me; *"You're just too nice, like all of the time and it's really frustrating dating a saint."*

A saint? A fucking saint!

Yep, that was a hard blow right in the gut and still to this very day makes my stomach clench painfully. He broke up with me because I'm too *nice*.

"Not in a good head space?" I repeat slowly and peel off the napkin laid out neatly over my lap. "You know what Trent, why don't you take all the time you need and while you do you can lose my number and go fuck yourself." I tell him and slap my napkin on the table as I push my chair back.

Trent stares at me, a startled look on his face as I rise from my seat. "Sav, please don't be upset. It's not you, baby doll, it's me, I'm the problem. You've always been a great girlfriend and the last thing I want to do is hurt you. I would like us to remain friends."

"Wow, friends?" I laugh bitterly and pick up my purse hanging on the back of the chair. "Here's to your *friendship*." I pick up my glass of Rioja and toss it over his crisp white, no doubt costly designer shirt. The exclusive five-star seafood restaurant we are currently dining in falls dead silent as the rest of the patrons watch me empty my over-priced glass of wine all over Trent. He gapes horrified down at his now wine-stained shirt.

"Cheers to all the bullshit excuses you've fed me over the last year. You truly are an abominable asshole." I utter placing the glass on the table and turning to walk out of the restaurant, ignoring the whispers and all the eyes in the restaurant that are following me as I exit.

I exhale when I walk out of the restaurant and bite back the tears that threaten to fall when my eyes prickle. I refuse to shed another tear for that fickle prick. I'm done with him for good his time. My friends are right, I've given him more chances than he deserves, and he has let me down with each one. I jump into one of the taxis waiting outside of the restaurant. "Sunrise Village, please." I tell the driver and he nods in response.

"Rough date?" He questions glancing back at me through the rear-view mirror.

"You could say that." I utter somberly and he smiles in understanding.

"Well, he must be a real tool to let a beautiful girl like you walk." He tells me and I force a smile on my face and keep my gaze out of the window.

It's no doubt that he is a tool, but I'm really starting to question whether there is something wrong with me? Was Trent right? Am I boring? My mother always told me; be the kind of girl your boyfriend would be proud to introduce to his mother. Trent never showed any intention of introducing me to his parents. I mean they're divorced, have been since Trent was a teenager I know that much, and he very briefly spoke about the broken relationship he has with his father, but he hasn't mentioned him since and I never pushed him to find out as it was clear he hasn't or refuses to deal with whatever issues he has with his family.

Nevertheless, he is no longer my problem.

"Hannah, am I boring?"

My best friend and roommate glances over at me quizzically from her cross-legged position on the sofa, the chopsticks full of noodles hovering over her mouth. "What? Of course you're not."

I swirl my own chopsticks through my Singapore noodles and sigh, "I can't stop wondering why Trent doesn't want to commit to me. Maybe I'm not adventurous enough for him and that's why he gets bored quickly. I mean he does keep mentioning how much of a good girlfriend I am and how I'm a saint. I don't understand how that could be a bad thing, you know? Since when has doting on your boyfriend been a bad thing?"

Hannah places her chopsticks in her box of noodles and licks her lips before she sighs. "Savi, please don't start questioning your qualities because of a moron like Trent. He's a narcissistic, mind-fucking, shit-head that has never been deserving of a great girl like you."

"What if he's right though Han? What if I am boring?" I argue, drop-ping my chopsticks in the box and setting it aside.

"You're not boring," Hannah presses trying her best to assure me but when I give her a dubious look she sighs and sets her box of noodles down too. "Okay, hear me out. Maybe, you're a conventional good girl who prefers to play on the safer side than take risks, and there's nothing wrong with that. Your wifey material, the type of girl that guys end up with after they have their fun, you know?"

My shoulders slump, "What you're trying to say is I'm the one they will eventually settle for. The loyal, good little housewife." I utter dryly. Hannah shakes her head and takes ahold of my hand, and she smiles warmly, her brown eyes like warm gooey chocolate gaze into mine.

"No babe, that's not what I mean at all. Girls like me, we're only worthy so long as we can provide a good time, but you, you're the one they choose to stay with forever."

I groan and cover my face with my hands. "Oh God, he is right. I'm too prim and predictable. Even in the bedroom, my preferred position is missionary for goodness' sake! It's not Trent's fault, it's mine! I have nothing interesting about me. I'm tedious and that's why he keeps dumping me!" I exclaim and get off the sofa to start pacing the small space of our living room. Hannah watches me with her dark brows knitted tightly. "You know what, no, I refuse to go down as the boring safe choice. I can be fun and carefree. I'm interesting and I'm going to show that good for nothing scoundrel how slutty I can really be. Get up girlfriend, we're going out."

Hannah blinks up at me, "Girlfriend?" she iterates.

I wince, "Yeah, I'm not cool enough to pull that one off, am I?"

THE 7 DAY STAND

Hannah laughs and shakes her head, "Sorry boo but no, in fact I'm going to do you a favor and forbid you from ever using that term again."

"Fine, get Vee up here too, I'm on a mission to get my slut on!"

That is my birthday wish. I said I didn't want to make a big fuss of my birthday, but fuck it, I'm determined to break out of this good girl persona that I've been involuntarily conditioned into by my parents.

I want to be a bad girl, no I *crave* to be and the first task on my list is to have a one-night stand with a hot stranger.

"SAVI, I'm all in favor of this new wild child mindset you're embracing, but are you absolutely sure about this?" Venice Di Luca my other bestie, my constant voice of reason and downstairs neighbor expresses as we clamber out of the Uber.

I spin and look at her, smoothing out the creases to my—or shall I say Hannah's— mini black dress I'm currently wearing. Probably the most revealing thing I've ever worn. I try to avoid wearing super short skirts because I find my legs are too short to pull them off. Sadly, I'm the short one within my friendship group while Hannah and Venice both stand at five foot nine I'm a meager five-foot-three.

"Absolutely and if you two get even the slightest whiff of me attempting to chicken out you remind me of that scallywag Trent's words, got it?" I tell them both firmly and they nod.

Hannah smiles and looks at the finger I'm pointing at them both. "We've got you, bitty boop." She chuckles and takes hold of my shoulders and turns me to face the entrance. "Now, stop yanking on that dress and walk like you have a purpose."

I wrinkle my nose, "Okay... but how does one walk with purpose?"

Venice rolls her eyes, "Firstly don't dawdle, you're sexy and confident. Walk into that bar like you own the place. Got it?"

I nod and blow a breath, "Got it, no dawdling, sexy and confident. I've got this." I take a step and almost buckle in the heels Venice forced me into wearing. Let me emphasize that I'm not the most graceful person at the best of times. I mean there have been instances where I've tripped over air, so these four-inch platform heels are lethal for me, but will I allow that to deter me? No sir-ee.

Onwards we shall go.

As we enter the bar the distinct smell of beer infused with a concoction of perfumes and aftershaves fills my senses. The bar isn't too crowded which makes it easy for us to maneuver through toward the LED lit circular bar situated to the far left of the stage with a karaoke setup where a group of girl friends are singing Britney Spears' "Wanna be". High tables and stools are dotted around the stage.

"What can I get you ladies?" The cute barman asks when we approach, tossing the cloth over his shoulder and placing his hands on the bar. I eye the impressive selection of spirits stacked around the bar. I drag my eyes back to the barman and observe him closely. The bar is far too dimly lit for me to see what color his eyes are, but I'm going to bet they're a deep dark brown. He's cute, a boyish grin spreads across his clean shaved face. He's a little too fresh-faced for my liking. I tend to favor guys with a stubble or beard and looking around I can spot a few.

"Can we have a round of blowjobs, please, sir?" My jaw drops and I look over at Venice pinning the barman with a sultry gaze. Oh boy. He seems to appreciate the innuendo dripping in her tone and nods, slowly licking his lips.

"You got it."

"I take it you're calling dibs on the barman?" Hannah asks with a smirk and Venice grins, her green eyes gleaming as her gaze follows him.

"Indeed, that's a tall glass of yumminess I can't wait to indulge in later." She gushes biting her lip and twirling a strand of her red hair between her fingers.

"Vee, how do you even know he's single?" I ask leaning against the bar. Venice looks over at me and shrugs.

"I didn't see no ring on his finger and a good-looking barman like that doesn't commit to just one girl, hun. I can guarantee you he has a different girl in his bed every night of the week."

"Really?" I sneak a look at the barman and let my eyes rake over him. Now that she mentions it, he does have that bad boy guise about him. I notice the long line of women draped across the bar batting their lashes waiting for him to notice them. "Wow, I'm so clueless about these things. Maybe this is a bad idea."

Hannah shoulder bumps me, "Nah ah, don't you go psyching yourself out of it, bitty. You can do this, you're one of the smartest girls I know. You just need some liquid courage and you'll be fine." She says just as our shots arrive.

"Ladies, your round of blowjobs *and* the screaming orgasms are on me." The barman states with a wink as he pushes the shot glasses toward us.

Venice smiles impishly at him, "That's rather bold, what if I don't like screaming orgasms?"

The barman throws his head back and laughs, "Then you clearly haven't had mine, gorgeous." He drawls, smiling charmingly, his dark eyes gleam with mischief. He leans in close to her, "Chase it down with the blowjob, you can thank me later."

Venice bites her lip and picks up her shot glass, her eyes never leaving his. Hannah and I share a knowing look. She smiles, pressing her shot glass to her lips. Jesus, I'm over here choking on their sexual chemistry turning ten different shades of red and she's grinning like the cat that caught the canary. "We'll see, hot shot."

"Oh bitty, don't look so flustered, drink up and let's go fishin' doll." Hannah teases me clearly noticing the pink tinge to my cheeks. We down the blowjobs and screaming orgasms and order another round of inappropriately named shots.

"Okay, now you order the drinks. Remember keep eye contact and give him a subtle flirtatious smile." Vee instructs me. I nod in understanding and hold up the empty shot glass and shudder after I down the shot of ass.

"I can't believe I just took a shot of delicious ass." I giggle drunkenly and the girl's cackle. "Hey, Jonas, get your sexy derrière over here and give me another shot of G-spot." Jonas, the bartender strolls over laughing. I snort and beckon him to lean closer so I could whisper to him, "My last boyfriend couldn't find his way to my G-spot with the help of a compass, the incompetent asshat. I bet you can though, you look like a man that knows his way around a woman's hoo-ha."

Jonah chuckles and pulls back to look at me, "Firstly your ex-boyfriend sounds like a real tool. Secondly, not only can I find your g-spot blindfolded and bound, I can also fuck you to multiple orgasms using just my tongue."

I gulp and stare at him dumbfounded, "Damn, with your *tongue?*" Jonah nods, flashing me a devious smirk that I'm sure has melted the panties off many women at this bar. "That's really a thing?"

Vee throws her arm around my shoulder and smiles coquettishly at Jonas, "Not only is it a thing, it's also fucking incredible my sexually thwarted friend."

I groan and look at my empty shot glass, "Oh God, my life is so depressing!"

"That's why we're here bitty, to change that and find you a man that's hungry and ready to devour that pussy." Hannah says handing me another shot of well at this point I don't even care what it is. I down the pink shot and shudder as the liquid burns on the way down.

"You're right let's go hunting. Oh, but first, I'm going to sing!" I exclaim and weave through the crowd toward the stage when the girl finally finishes butchering 'A Thousand Miles' by Vanessa Carlton.

I shuffle through the songs on the playlist and smile when I see the classic, 'I Hate Myself for Loving You' by Joan Jett & The Blackhearts.

Hell, if that isn't fitting.

Thank the lord for the alcohol swimming in my system because there isn't usually a force on this earth that will get me up on stage let alone sing.

The song starts and the dazzlingly bright spotlight comes on as I slowly lift my gaze to the crowded bar, every single pair of eyes in the room watching me.

Oh crap.

Chapter 3

Savi

I Hate Myself For Loving You - Joan Jett & The Black Hearts

COME ON SAVI, now's not the time to choke. You can do this, just start singing. This one is for you, Trent Lane.

The heat of the spotlight beaming down on me, the lack of air-conditioning paired with the alcohol in my body is making me perspire. I can feel every thump of the bass under my feet. My throat goes bone dry. My eyes find Venice and Hannah as they move to stand at the front of the stage. They nod encouragingly and I exhale and somehow the lyrics start falling out of my mouth.

The crowd start to cheer and sing along with me which helps rid the nerves fluttering around wildly in my belly. By the second verse of the song, I was singing my heart out. Microphone in hand I'm dancing my way through the crowd singing. My gaze locks with a pair of piercing grey eyes across the room and I almost forget the lyrics to the song and the ability to breathe.

Slowly I make my way over to his table and he watches me intently. All of my natural instincts scream at me to back away, but I can't fight the pull that is drawing me to him. "I think of you every night and day, you took my heart, and you took my pride away," I sing the lyrics to him, and he watches me, the corner of his lip quirks ever so slightly.

I circle around him, my finger lightly trailing over the exposed flesh of his forearm where the sleeves of his shirt have been rolled up to his elbows displaying part of his tattoo. Those molten eyes of his follow me fervently and I keep mine on his while I sing and slowly back away toward the stage.

The song comes to an end, and we've yet to break eye contact. The loud cheer and applause from the crowd broke me out of the trance this gloriously beautiful yet mysterious man has sucked me into.

"Oh my God, Savi that was so awesome!" Hannah squeals, hugging me. I tear my eyes away from his and laugh as the girls drag me back toward the bar.

"You absolutely rocked it babe, I'm so proud of you. See, you're a total badass!" Vee gushes with a grin and orders us another round of drinks. I'm sure it's the alcohol I have flowing through my veins, but my body is thrumming with this uncontrollable exhilaration. After taking all those shots, I'm suddenly feeling rather sober. My stomach however protests the idea of having any more alcohol.

"Girls, my God, that honestly felt so... nerve-wracking yet invigorating all at the same time." I admit with a chuckle. "Holy crap, did you see that guy. When I walked over to him my heart almost tore right through my chest it was beating so hard and fast. Seriously girls, how drunk am I? I'm not imagining him right, he really is *that* hot?"

"Hell yes he is. Savi, the man hasn't been able to take his eyes off you since," Hannah tells me with a girlish grin. "If you still want to play on the wild side, why not go over there and... kiss him?" I gape at her wide-eyed.

"What?" I stammer and shake my head. "Don't be ridiculous, I can't do that."

"Why not?" Vee jumps in. "He's clearly interested, he's practically eye-fucking you from across the room." She justifies and I chew my bottom lip contemplatively.

He is? Before I could stop myself my eyes veer over to him and sure enough, he is still watching me. My belly warms when the corner of his lip quirks while he continues watching me.

"Well, for starters he's clearly older than me, what if he's married or in a relationship? I can't just go and plant my lips on a guy I don't even know." I defend but they both just stare at me blankly.

"First of all, older guys are way better in bed." Vee states with a chef's kiss. "Secondly, Savi, the entire reason for us coming out tonight was for that specific purpose, remember? I can sniff out a man that knows his way around a woman and babe, that tall glass on sin right there is your guy. If you're not going for him in the next five minutes, I will." She finishes and leans into my ear, a devious smirk on her beautiful face. "I dare you."

A drink is set down before me in a tall glass, Jonas smiles handsomely, "It seems you've caught someone's attention. This is for you...it's called *foreplay*." He says and looks over my shoulder in the direction of the silver fox.

"Well, if that isn't a clear sign he's interested, I don't know what is." Hannah states grinning at me wildly.

I swallow thickly, my throat suddenly bone dry. I pick up the drink and lean my back against the bar while I take a slow sip, keeping my eyes on his. The liquid burns on the way down and I shudder a little. The rim of the glass is coated with a purple sugar that instinctively has me licking my lips and I almost moan against the sweet and sour taste. *What is that?*

"Mm, oh my God, this is delicious," I coo taking another sip. Jonas leans against the bar near my ear and speaks softly.

"The sugar on the rim mixed with the drink makes you want to constantly lick your lips, craving more of that sweet yet tangy taste...

hence the name *foreplay*." He explains. "Trust me, take a sip of that just before you kiss him and watch him devour your mouth."

Okay, I can do this. I'm fearless. I'm a confident, intelligent woman. "Here goes nothing," I utter and before I lose my nerve I walk over to his table. I take a sip of the drink as I approach him. The silver fox's eyes find and hold mine, they narrow while he watches me walking the short distance toward him over the rim of the glass as he also takes a long sip of his drink.

As I approach him, he spins a little on his stool, so his body is facing me directly. His entire demeanor just exudes confidence and I'd be lying if that didn't moisten my panties that much more. He has one foot resting on the ground and the other is perched up on the metal footrest. I couldn't focus on anything around me but him and the intent look he held in his eyes. My stomach tenses a little more with each step and before my brain could process and impede my idiocy or talk me out of it my lips are latched onto his.

Oh, sweet lord.

I couldn't explain what I felt in that moment if my life depended on it. All I can focus on is the silkiness of his lips against mine and the feel of his stubble scratching my chin, oh and the low groan that emits from him. I'm aware this is going to sound bizarre and so incredibly cliché, but it almost feels as though my lips were made just for him.

The first two seconds we both go stock still, even though *I* kissed *him* I'm just as stunned as he likely is. I can't believe I did it. My eyes are closed, I don't dare open them in fear of being met with a stormy glare. Nevertheless, even with my eyes closed, I can still sense him staring at me. His chiseled jaw ticks under my hands where I have them placed on either side of his face.

Shit. Shit. Shit.

What if he's mad? This is going to be awkward.

I start to draw back and just as I do, he gently catches my lower lip between his teeth. A quiet moan inadvertently escapes me when he sucks on my lip teasingly. I feel his hand come up and grip my hip, he draws me between his legs while his tongue dexterously sneaks into my mouth seeking out my own. If it wasn't for the tight grip that he has on me, I would honestly melt into a puddle right there between his legs.

Fireworks explode behind my eyelids when our tongues sensually glide over one another. The taste of him and the whiskey he's been drinking combined is simply intoxicating. He kisses me with long and commanding strokes of his tongue that leaves my mind as well as my limbs weak.

Everyone and everything but the two of us quickly disappears. My hand moves from his jaw to the nape of his neck, my fingers find and stroke the fuzzy short hair at the base of his neck as our kiss deepens. The gesture causes a deep throaty groan of gratification to emit from him which then cascades right through me.

Oh, sweet heavens, I want more of that sound. I want more of *him*.

Regrettably my lungs eventually start to burn from lack of oxygen, so we slowly pull apart, panting. My eyes open at the same time as his and we gaze at one another. Protruding, intelligent grey eyes stare back at me curiously. Jeez, his eyes are even more beautiful up close. A deep grey with flecks of hazel laced with dark lashes.

"Well damn," he drawls and stops to lick his lips before he speaks again. "Damn, drink that good, was it?" Oh boy, even his voice is sexy. All smoky and husky, but not in that croaky hoarse type of way, oh no, he speaks in a controlled and confident manner.

My cheeks burn red hot under his gaze, and I chuckle veering my gaze from his, "It was actually, thank you."

He licks his lips, "Do you go around kissing every man that buys you a drink?" He questions, narrowing his eyes while he pushes a loose strand of my hair away from my face. My mouth drops open and when I feel his fingers brush against my cheek, I have to suppress the overwhelming urge to lean into it.

"No, I don't." I reply, practically breathless. "That was definitely a first for me."

A dark brow goes up and I detect a ghost of a smirk. "Well, in that case darling, I'm flattered," he expresses coolly, and, in that moment, it dawns on me that we're still in a rather intimate position. I'm standing between his deliciously thick, muscular thighs and his hand is still on my hip while mine is draped around his neck, our faces so close our noses are practically touching. "You're not on a girls gone wild bachelorette party, are you?"

I gape at him wide-eyed. "What?"

He gestures with his head toward Hannah and Venice watching us with wide grins spread across both their faces. "Are you getting married?"

I shake my head so fast I make myself dizzy, "God no. It's my birthday, I'm out celebrating my birthday with my friends, and they dared me to kiss you, so I did."

Silver fox's brows pinch together, and he watches me intently for a moment looking like he wants to say something but thinks better of it. "That's rather brazen of you. What if I'm spoken for?"

Oh shit, *is he* spoken for? The thought alone of him having a girl-friend or wife stirs a jealousy in me I know I have no business feeling. I don't even know this man, "Are you?" I ask, removing my hand from his neck and shifting to back away. The grip he has on my hip disap-pears when he snakes his arms around my waist and hauls me up against him.

I gasp, surprised and silver fox smiles wolfishly. My eyes are instantly drawn to his mouth when he licks his lips and I'm inwardly longing for those lips to be on mine again. "Maybe."

There's a roguish glint in his eyes and I exhale when I realize he's teasing me. "Well, you certainly didn't kiss me like you're spoken for." I point out and his eyes instantly drop to my lips, and he bites down on his bottom lip.

19

"How did I kiss you?" he asks lowly.

"Ravenously." I answer, with absolutely zero hesitation. I think I'm starting to get the hang of this whole flirting thing. "Like a man that's been left to starve and is served his favorite meal and wants to savor every taste."

"A taste as sinful as yours is hard to resist."

Not as sinful as your lips.

Those words almost slip right out of my mouth, but I catch myself just in time. That's a little too forward, or is it? Oh, screw it, if what I have in my head doesn't go as I'm hoping then I'll never see him again anyway. I couldn't tear my eyes from his, the way he's looking at me with such fervor has me transfixed. "Something tells me you're no stranger to sin, Mr...?" I purr looking up at him through my lashes.

The look of surprise that flashes across his face fleetingly suggests that he wasn't expecting me to be so forward. My breath hitches in my throat as I wait for his response.

His smirk is cocky as he looks over my face, "Pierce." He tells me steadily, "Logan Pierce." Tingles ripple up and down my spine when his large hand enfolds around the back of my thigh. I feel the heat of his hand rapidly spread through me and coil between my legs. With an inward groan I press my legs together.

Fuck, even his name is insanely attractive.

I watch him intently as he slowly slides his hand higher up my leg, his grey eyes glitter wickedly under the florescent lighting of the bar. "This is where you tell me your name, sweetheart."

"Savannah West." I force out and swallow against the sudden dryness of my throat when his fingers brush against my gluteal fold. I'm vaguely aware that we are in a bar full of people, and he has his hand up my skirt, but I do nothing to stop him. Logan stares down into my eyes, his thumb drawing lazy circles over my heated flesh which causes my pulse to jump with every deliberate stroke.

"Savannah," he repeats and I almost swoon right there at the way my name just rolls off his tongue. My eyes close when he leans in, his lips narrowly missing mine to whisper in my ear. "I bet you taste as intoxicating as you smell, Savannah." I visibly quiver against the heat of his breath on my ear and a breathy moan escapes me. "And you're right, I'm absolutely no stranger to *all* things sin, and right now, sweetheart, all I can think about is how my name will sound on your lips, when I sit you on my face and lick that sweet cunt of yours to orgasm," he boldly declares in my ear.

Holy *fuck*.

An unappeasable heat swarms my entire body. I'm burning with utmost desire from the inside out. My knees tremble perilously like they're about to give out on me while my clit flutters and pulses like it has its own damn heartbeat and he's not even touched me yet.

What is this spell this ridiculously fine-looking man has me under? And why am I so eager to hear more of him whispering such vulgarity to me. God, he smells so good I almost bury my nose into the crook of his neck just to savor the scent. The woody yet citrusy notes of his aftershave only amplify my current state of arousal. When Logan pulls back to look at me, he keeps his eyes on my mouth and I'm sure he's deliberating whether to kiss me or not, so I wait for him to close the gap between our lips, but he doesn't. Instead, he draws back a little and my stomach sinks with disappointment.

Will I allow that little snag to deter me? Absolutely not. I'm throwing out the rule book tonight and jumping headfirst right out of my comfort zone.

You can do this Sav, you can be sexy. Every woman has that sultriness buried deep inside her, just tap into yours. I let my eyes leisurely rake over his gorgeous face, "If ever there was a face made to be sat on, it would without a shadow of a doubt be yours." I voice sensually and inch a little closer. "Though, I think it's only fair I warn you that I'm not a girl that's easily satisfied."

Logan's lips curl into a knowing smirk and the challenge that ignites in those grey eyes doesn't go unnoticed by me. His free hand comes up and he grips my chin, tilting my head up slightly. "Do I look like the type of man that would allow a girl to leave his bed unsatisfied, darling?" he drawls, his thumb tracing the outline of my lower lip. "One night with me and not only will I fuck every one of those losers you've slept with before me out of your system. I'll also make certain that you'll be incapable of walking straight for days."

Jeezus, I have never in my life burned so hot for a man. I'd let him have his way with me right here and now in the middle of the bar what with the way my pussy is pulsating lasciviously between my legs.

"Why are we still standing here?" I ask him brazenly and he wets his lips, the corner of his eyes crinkle slightly while staring into mine. "Take me home, Logan Pierce and show me what I've been missing."

Damn, just saying those words felt outlandish to me, but goodness the ravenous look on his face had me feeling some type of way I've never felt before. I'm nervous and excited all at the same time and I'm unsure what to focus on, my breathing or the incessant throbbing between my legs.

Logan's fingers move from my chin and dance over my collarbone and curl at the nape of my neck. A surprised gasp escapes me when he grips my nape tight and draws my face closer to his, his lips brush along my cheek before they brush against the shell of my ear when he speaks to me in a low gruff tone. "Are you sure you're ready for what you're getting yourself into, sweetheart?"

No. I'm not, but if there is one thing I'm certain about, it's that I want every delectable inch of him pressed against me and there is no denying the flaming desire I have coursing through my body for this magnetic force of a man.

"We won't know if we keep standing around here now, will we?" I tell him gallantly, and when he draws back a touch and peers down into my face, almost as if he's searching for reassurance or any sign of doubt, I inch closer, my lips almost grazing his. "I'm bursting to strip you out of these clothes and explore every inch of what you've got hiding under all these layers of clothing, Mr Pierce, because from what I can see it will certainly not disappoint."

Logan smiles and his thumb strokes the back of my neck, "Want to know what I'm dying for sweetheart? To feel your nails clawing wildly at my back when I pin your knees by your ears and fuck you savagely until you're begging me to stop."

"What if I don't want you to stop?"

"Then we'll keep going." He affirms, his lips grazing the length of my neck. "Until we're both spent and pass the fuck out." My eyes close and I sway on my feet, my head swims with irrepressible desire, my panties now completely soaked through. "The immoral things I'll do to you will taint your purity, darlin'." A lustful moan pushes past my lips when he sinks his teeth into my neck, biting with just enough force to send a jolt of pleasure rippling straight to my core before he runs his tongue over it.

I smile and draw my head back a little so I could look at him. "As long as you taint me using that mouth, I'm all in, Mr Pierce." I purr, feeling daring I drag my index finger along his jaw.

Logan stares at me, smiling handsomely. "Oh, I plan to use more than just my mouth, sweetheart." He drops a couple of hundred-dollar bills on the table and rises from his bar stool and I crane my neck to peer up at him.

Fuck, he's tall. I mean, truth be told most people are when compared to my tiny ass, but I didn't pay much attention to how long his legs were until he is stood at his full height. "I'm going to tell my friends that I'm leaving really quick and meet you by the exit."

Logan nods and his eyes very briefly veer over my shoulder to Hannah and Venice standing by the bar flirting shamelessly with two guys, one of them being Logan's friend that he arrived with. "It seems our friends are too occupied getting acquainted to concern themselves with our absences."

I chuckle and nod looking over at my friends rather content with their company, "I think you might be right," I should go over there and tell them I'm leaving; it would probably be the sensible thing to do, however the heat from Logan's hand pressed to the base of my back has me more than eager to leave this bar with him. Those whispered promises of what he plans to do to me and the thrill of not knowing what will happen after we leave this bar has the confined, wayward girl squirming animatedly inside of me.

It's such a bizarre feeling to be so eager to go off with a stranger, but I feel oddly comfortable and safe with him. There's just something so calming about his presence that quietens any doubts I have. "Shall we?" he questions before he leans in close to my ear, "Every second we waste standing here sweetheart is one second less I get to spend feasting on your pussy."

My eyes close and heat rushes up my neck straight up to my face and I feel my pulse race that little bit faster in response to the wickedness of his tone. "Lead the way," I reply, peering up at him when he draws back.

Logan flashes me a knee weakening smile revealing an undereye dimple just below his left eye. I didn't even know dimples under the eye were a thing till I saw his and sweet heavens when I tell you it only accentuated his sex appeal. My legs eagerly follow him toward the exit whilst my brain is busy absorbing the feel of his strong fingers lacing with mine as we weave through the crowd of people in the bar.

We walk out of the bar and Logan leads me toward a matte, gun metal Ferrari convertible. I'm no whizz when it comes to car models but looking at this car, I would say it costs more than I'll ever make in my lifetime... twice over.

I stare at him as he reaches over and pulls the car door open for me. It's clear he's wealthy if the car, his Rolex, and the stylish attire he's wearing is any indication. I can't help but wonder why or how he wound up in a dive like Q's. A man as affluent as he seems to be surely would choose to be in some luxurious cocktail bar in Gaslamp quarter.

I marvel at the way his crisp powder blue shirt stretches across the luscious muscles of his strapping back.

My oh my.

Logan straightens and turns to look at me while he holds the door open. "Not too late to change your mind, sweetheart." He voices tranquilly, licking his lips, those silver eyes penetratingly hold my gaze. I don't hesitate and walk the short distance between us, my eyes never leaving his as I saunter past him to the passenger side and slide into the plush, red leather seat.

I catch the short nod and the lift of his lip just before he pushes the door shut and walks around the car to get in. I inhale, filling my lungs with oxygen to ease the nerves knotting deep in my belly. There's a hint of his aftershave mixed with the distinct smell of leather as soon as I get into the car.

Logan pushes a button and the car roars to life. The beast-like rumble of the engine vibrates and travels through my already heated body and when Logan turns and pins me with a sidelong look full of waywardness, I press my thighs together and quickly swallow the moan that almost escapes me. It's the promise he holds behind his gaze and the anticipation of what's to come that has me squirming in the leather seat of his half a million-dollar car.

Logan leans across the centre console, his lips grazing along my jaw till he reaches the shell of my ear, "Keep that cunt nice and wet for me sweetheart because I'm going to spend the night making you cum in ways you never thought possible."

Holy... freaking... shit.

Chapter 4
Logan

◦——♡——◦

Same Place - JOY

I'M A BAD MAN.

Logan Pierce, what in the shit is wrong with you?

I'm a forty-year-old man sat in a bar lusting after a girl probably twenty years my junior.

Oh, to be twenty-one again. And had I been, by now, I'd have had her on her knees with that pretty mouth of hers wrapped around my dick while I throat fucked her till she's crying.

Goddamn, there are plenty of women in this bar more suitable for me, but my fucking eyes keep veering over to her standing by the bar conversing with her friends.

The moment she walked into Q's my eyes zeroed in on her laughing with her two girlfriends. I can't tell you how, but I somehow knew she was coming before she even walked in through the door. I'm truly dumbstruck, sat here trying to conjure up the words to describe the way my body reacted when I first saw her.

Her long and sleek golden blonde hair blows back as she pushes the door open and walks in followed closely by her two friends. She's petite, no taller than five-foot three at most and I'm surprised because for such a small thing her presence fills the rooms almost instantly stifling me. I can hear my buddy Jack talking to me rather animatedly about something that happened at work earlier, but my brain isn't registering a single fucking word that is flying out of his mouth. Every sound around me becomes distant and indistinct—everything but the sound of her melodious laugh. The vibrant and melodic sound resonates right through me, and I immediately crave more of it.

When she got up on that stage to sing and those amber eyes found mine in the crowd there wasn't a force on this earth strong enough to compel me to look away. I watched enthralled as she sang the lyrics to 'I Hate Myself for Loving You' by Joan Jett and the Blackhearts.

A classic.

She has great taste in music, and I like that.

My attraction for this striking young woman was instantaneous and unlike anything I've ever experienced in my life, and I've had my share of relationships, some I wouldn't even deem as such simply because they didn't last long enough for it to develop into one. The longest relationship I've had was with April... my ex-wife and the mother of my son. I gave that malicious woman nineteen years of my life and all she did was suck the life out of me for every single fucking one of them. Had I gotten an inkling of what a manipulative and possessive shrew she really was back then I would have turned and ran as fast and far as humanly possible, but she hid her true colours well, at least until she got pregnant, and we were fast tracked to marriage.

After the experience I had with her I got a vasectomy and swore off marriage. We've been divorced for almost eight years now and we're both happier for it. Well, I can't speak for her but shit, I certainly am. Though she spent the better half of the eight years relentlessly poisoning and turning my son against me and of course, he chose to buy into all her bullshit stories which has resulted in a breakdown in our relationship. She filled his head with lies, telling him that I was abusive with her, I was a neglectful husband and unfaithful to her.

All fucking lies. I've never cheated, despite having the opportunity to do so on countless occasions I remained faithful to her until I took the ring off my finger and signed the divorce papers.

I'm determined to rebuild that severed bond with him and I'll keep trying—despite that wench's best effort I will get my kid back but that's a matter for another day, right now my attention is firmly fixed on the beautiful girl squirming in the passenger seat beside me.

Fucking Christ, I can't remember ever being this eager to fuck a woman in my life. The sweet and tangy scent of her perfume or whatever product she currently has on is scrambling my brain to a point I'm finding myself fighting the urge to pull this car over, straddle her perfect peachy ass over my lap and feed my cock into her pussy.

I lean across, my lips skimming along the silk flesh of her jaw till I reach the shell of her ear, "Keep that cunt nice and wet for me sweetheart because I'm going to spend the night making you cum in ways you never thought possible." I vow gruffly in her ear and smile when I feel her quiver ever so slightly.

Savannah turns her head slightly to look at me when I start to draw back. My eyes drop to the soft pillow of those divine lips of hers which she has clasped between her teeth. I almost lean in to suck on her lower lip but much to my disappointment the traffic light turns green, so I'm forced to pull away and resume driving, the impatient asshole behind me has already begun flashing and beeping at me to get a move on. Talk about ruining the damn moment.

The drive to my Condo took no more than thirty minutes. It's late and for a change the roads are oddly empty for a Friday night. "So..." she starts and stops to clear her throat before continuing. "What do you do for a living?" Savannah questions, her eyes flittering across the interior of my car, rightfully curious how I can afford a half a million-dollar car.

"I work in construction."

"You *work* in construction?" She iterates dubiously, her brows rising slightly. The apparent incredulity in her tone makes me chuckle. I turn to glance at her fleetingly before turning my attention to the road again. "My knowledge of cars is shockingly minimal, but even I know a construction *worker* doesn't earn nearly enough to afford a *Ferrari*."

"That is a valid point, but did you consider the possibility that it might be a rental?" I reply flippantly and she smiles back at me, her eyes glittering with mirth as they rake over me.

"No, that's highly unlikely given the way you dress and the expensive watch on your wrist. No, you give off the executive vibe. A director perhaps?"

I smirk and wet my lips, my thumb brushing over her knuckles. "An executive vibe? Is that you politely calling me a snob?"

Savannah's eyes grow wide, and her jaw goes slack with surprise while she stares at me like an adorable deer caught in headlights. "No," she hurries to elucidate. "Not at all. I just meant that you have the persona of an executive. Your characteristics and the way you carry yourself it's easy to envision you in an authoritative role."

That lovely pink flush that creeps into her cheeks makes my dick throb and ache in my slacks.

I must admit though, I'm impressed, she clearly has good instinctual perception and that's rare nowadays. And knowing she's been closely observing me pleases me more than I care to admit. I may just have to make damn certain I give her an unforgettable taste of just how authoritative I can be.

The rest of the journey we conversed about random things. I told her that I started my own company after I graduated from Stanford university using the seed capital my father invested to help me get my company off its feet. Savannah went on to share that she is currently working as an apprentice for Glitz and Glam events hoping to get enough experience in event organising to eventually start her own company.

She's not only intuitive and beautiful she's also highly ambitious. The passion and excitement that exudes from her when she's talking about planning events is truly admirable. I'm very familiar with Glitz and Glam, we've used their services in the past, most recently being the charity black tie gala a year ago. Susan Saunders is the director of the company; our fathers used to golf together.

The conversation flows effortlessly between us, no awkward silences and while I listen to her it's slowly dawning on me that I've not spent this long talking to a woman—and *enjoying it* in a very long time.

The last sexual encounter I had was six months ago in Paris when I was away for a conference.

Damn. Has it really been that long?

To be completely honest I've barely had time to breathe lately between work and all the travelling I've had to do. Not to mention I've not met anyone, nor had any desire to... until tonight. Savannah is the first woman to catch my attention in a long time and even that encounter with... fuck I don't even recall her name—well, that absolutely sums up that experience. It was monotonous at best, more of a necessity to ease off some tension, though truth be told I would have gotten much more gratification fucking my fist.

"You live on the *beach*?" Savannah questions her hazel eyes wide as we pull up to my beachfront condo.

"Occasionally," I answer, pushing the button and killing the engine. "I have a place in the city. I only come here when I need to escape the chaos of the city and I'm in desperate need of some peace and quiet to recharge."

"Wow," she breathes, veering her gaze toward the ocean stretched out before her, a serene look falls upon her pretty face. It's the middle of the night, but the view is just as incredible and even more tranquil. The moonlight reflects on the surface of the water accompanied by glittering stars littered across the sky. "It's beautiful. This right here would be my idea of heaven."

"I like it here. Have you ever been for a midnight swim?" I question and Savannah turns to look at me and shakes her head slowly. "Well, we must rectify that immediately. Come on."

Savannah blanches, golden eyes all wide and panicked. "Wait, *now*? I don't have a bathing suit."

I smile, taking hold of her chin I gaze into her eyes as I stroke my thumb along her jaw. "Who said you need one? There isn't a soul around but the two of us. The couple that lives in the condo at the end over there have already flown out to Florida for the summer to see their kids and the rest are rentals."

"So, you're proposing we go skinny dipping at..." she voices and stops to glance over at the clock on the center console. "...one thirty in the morning?"

Smirking I inch closer until my lips are less than a breath apart from hers. "Precisely. You can swim, can't you?" I question, slipping the spaghetti strap of her dress off her shoulder using my index finger.

"Yes, I can swim." She answers breathily, her velvet lips parting for me when I teasingly graze mine over hers. I can sense the apprehension coming off her in waves since we left the bar. As much as she's trying to convince herself that she's the type of girl that sleeps around, she's not. I've had a catalogue of promiscuous women in my time and Savannah isn't one of those girls, not even close. If I had to guess I'd say she's only slept with a handful of men at most, each one likely incompetent at pleasuring her in the bedroom. I could taste her purity the moment she walked into Q's which is why I was surprised when she waltzed over and kissed me.

Nevertheless, I want more. I want to taint her. I want to be the one to make every sordid fantasy she has a reality. I want to corrupt her mind, so I'm all she thinks and fantasizes about.

"Good, now let go of that last thread of doubt in your mind and leave yourself to me, Savannah." I say pushing the other strap down until her shoulders are bare. "Tonight, I want you to be mine completely, no doubts, no hesitation, only mine."

31

"Okay." She assents softly, her eyes closed, and lips still parted patiently waiting for me to close the miniscule gap and kiss her and fuck am I aching to taste those lips, but I know if I do, I'll lose the very last bit of control I have left and pull her in my lap and fuck her till she's screaming.

"Say it."

"Only yours."

"Good girl," I praise, my tone low and deep. My wandering fingers find the zipper to her dress, and I slowly unfasten it and as I do the dress loosens before the material slides off the top half of her body, revealing the navy blue, *lace*, strapless bra she's wearing underneath.

Lord have mercy I'm having to fight the urge to tear it off with my bare teeth just so I could suck at the budding nipple under the lace material. There are simply no words to describe the crass things I want to do to this woman, the countless ways I would like to defile her. "Step out of the car, sweetheart and lose the dress. Let me see you." Savannah complies and obediently opens the car door and steps out, my eyes eagerly following her every movement. Like a depraved sex maniac, my mouth salivates when the hem of her mini dress rides up exposing smooth, creamy skin and the delectable curve of her ass. I follow suit, walking around the car toward her, watching eagerly as the dress slips over her hips, then her toned legs and eventually pools at her feet.

Fuck me.

There she stands before me in nothing but her lace bra and matching panties— and those sexy black stilettos. My step falters ever so slightly as I reach her, my eyes leisurely roam over every inch, storing every dip and curve of her perfect body into my memory bank for later because the sight before me is not one I want to forget in a hurry. "Goddamn Savannah, you're fucking unreal."

Savannah's eyes that are cast down the entire time snap up and she stares back at me stunned as if hearing those words for the very first time. I don't even need to ask because with every passing second, it's becoming more and more apparent that she's been mistreated in her past relationships.

Those fools she's dated in the past without a doubt robbed her of her self-esteem which is a darn shame because she's outstandingly beautiful and deserves so much better. And I plan to give her a taste of how it feels to be treasured, to be taken care of, to be *owned*. I grip her narrow hips and draw her up against me, immediately relishing the way her body feels pressed up against mine.

"This isn't very fair, I'm practically naked and you're still fully clothed," she purrs with a teasing smile, "I think we should even out the playing field a little, don't you?"

I match her smile but say nothing when her hands come up and she slowly unbuttons my shirt, pushing one button out of its loop at a time. I watch her, gauging her reaction closely and God, the red-hot desire that glitters in her eyes with every inch of exposed flesh makes my groin tighten. Especially the way she's biting down on her lower lip. I sigh when her fingers skim down the length of my torso, her fingertips lightly tracing the outline of my abs. I take hold of her wrists and her eyes snap up to meet mine. "If you keep touching me like that, we're not going to make it to the beach or the bedroom. I will spread you out on the hood of my car and fuck you till you're screaming for mercy."

Savannah smiles impishly, unbuttons my pants and slowly unfastens the zipper. My cock throbs and my hips instinctively rock up into her touch. "So far, all I'm hearing is talk, Mr. Pierce." She states, raising a challenging brow. "When are you planning to put your words to action?"

"So eager to be fucked. I bet your pretty cunt is aching to be stretched out and pumped full of my hot cum." I growl hooking an arm under her peachy ass and lifting her effortlessly into my arms. Savannah's legs coil around me and she rocks herself against me and moans. "That's it sweetheart, rub your clit up and down my cock, keep that pussy plump and juicy for me." Savannah moans again and continues to grind herself against me while I walk up to the house. I don't even know how I managed to get up those steps, find my keys and unlock the door with our mouths fused, kissing ardently and fuck the way Savannah is dry humping my dick is absolute torture; with each thrust of her hips she's pushing me to the edge of insanity.

My fingers travel up from the nape of her neck to curl in her hair. I grip the roots and tug her head back so I can bite and suck at her throat emitting a melodious moan from Savannah.

"Logan..."

My body responds to her call; that all too familiar surge of heat rushes through me and pools deep in my groin. There is no way we're making it to the bedroom, so I kick away the chair and swipe off various contents I have on the marble dining table and set Savannah on top of it. I grip her nape and draw her mouth urgently to mine and I kiss her hard and deep swallowing every one of her hushed moans. While we kiss our hands are occupied undressing one another. Savannah pulls my shirt off and her dainty hands roam free exploring my chest closely, followed by her mouth licking a trail from my pecs up to my throat, stopping to suck at the base of my neck.

"Fuck." I groan audibly, tilting my head back to give her more space to continue peppering open mouthed kisses along my throat. My control is waning, and I can feel that untamable beast clawing its way to the surface despite my grandest effort to keep him at bay.

I find the back strap to her bra and with one firm tug I tear it open freeing those glorious c-cup tits. Savannah gasps and looks down at her bare tits and then back up at me watching as I drop her now torn bra on the floor.

"Lean back." I command raspingly, dragging my thumb over a hardened nipple and pinching with just enough pressure that she whimpers. "I want you to tell me if I'm too rough with you, understand?" Savannah nods and lays back, her chest rising and falling quickly, full lips slightly parted, and cheeks a pretty shade of pink.

Fuck me, she's a sight.

Our eyes interlock and I keep my gaze on hers while I slowly drag my fingertips up her thighs leaving a trail of goosebumps in my wake until I reach the waistband of her panties and tear them off, leaving her completely bare for me.

I take a step back and press her underwear to my nose and inhale her scent while she watches me with wide lustful eyes. It's astounding how she can look so sweet and innocent yet so unbelievably seductive at the same time.

I'm torn between wanting to take a moment to admire and burn the image of her perfect body wet and ready into my memory bank, but the impatient part of me is burning to feed my throbbing cock deep into her tantalizingly glistening cunt.

"I want to see you," Savannah voices leaning up on her elbows. I waste no time in giving her what she wants. I kick my shoes off and remove my pants and boxers all in one go. Savannah's eyes lower to my rock hard eight-inch dick standing to attention, the tip glistening with pre-cum.

Savannah licks her lips and swallows thickly before she lifts her eyes to look at me and says, "Oh... it's *pierced*."

I smile and move over to her, taking hold of her ankle I pull her shoes off and press an open-mouthed kiss to her calf. "It sure is. Never experienced a pierced dick before I take it?" Savannah shakes her head slowly and watches me closely as I kiss my way up her inner thigh. "Good." I utter gripping her hips, I tug her to the edge of the dining table. "Lay back baby and allow me to demonstrate the many benefits a pierced cock has to offer..."

Chapter 5
Savi

Woo x I Was Never There remix - Untrusted, Creamy , (Tiktok version)

I CANNOT BELIEVE I'm doing this.

My heart jack hammers against my ribs as I lay completely naked before a man— *a very sexy man*—I know absolutely nothing about. A man whose grey eyes are staring into my soul while his head descends between my legs. His lips inching closer and closer to my pussy which is fluttering zealously in anticipation.

"You have such a pretty pussy, Savannah," Logan groans kissing the pubic area of my sex, his eyes never leaving mine. Well shit, this is a first, no one has ever referred to my vagina as pretty before. I make a mental note to thank Yazmin, my beauty therapist, for keeping things pretty *down under* for me.

I quiver inwardly in response to not only his words, but the ravening look he holds in his gaze. My body heats and my hips instinctively roll up mutely urging him to where I need him. His lips move in a deliberate and teasing manner, nipping and licking everywhere but where I'm burning to have him. "Logan..." I gasp when his tongue glides through my folds and sweeps across my clit making me visibly shudder. I can't remember the last time I had my pussy eaten but I know it's been a very long time, so much so that the sensations of that one lick sent shockwaves of pleasure rippling through me. My legs quiver and go to close when his lips close over my clit and he sucks, but Logan's hands move from hips to my thighs, spreading them wider with a firm grip to keep them open.

"Oh God..." I cry out, my fingers curl in his hair when he flicks his tongue quicker and firmer against my clit. Whatever Logan is doing to me has my body quaking and convulsing in a way it never has before. The sexy low groans and appreciative noises emitting from him while he devours me only fuels my pleasure, and once my body adjusts and I'm no longer sensitive to his ministrations my body moves on its own, matching his rhythm. I'm grinding myself wildly against that dexterous tongue desperate for that release.

I've never had an orgasm from oral sex and penetration was always a hit and miss with my past boyfriends. Unfortunately, I fall in the small percentage of women that doesn't orgasm easily, well, unless I'm pleasuring myself, and most of the time my partners simply didn't have the endurance to hold back until I was ready nor the technique to take me over.

The closest I've gotten was with Trent, he was the best out of the bunch, at least he tried to get me there. Yet, for some strange reason my body wouldn't allow me to go over the edge and reach an orgasm.

Even now I'm desperate to go over, I can feel it, taste it even but just as I hit that point the pressure becomes too much and however hard I try I just can't seem to push past that wall.

"Savannah, eyes on me." Logan utters between licks. I force my eyes open and look at him panting. "I'm going to be down here until you cum for me. I don't care if it takes all fucking night. I'm going to drink up that orgasm sweetheart." He asserts and keeps his eyes firmly on mine as he runs the tip of his tongue over my engorged clit with kittenish licks. "You're right there but you're tensing baby, just relax and let your body do its thing."

"God, I can't." I pant, shaking my head in frustration. "I've never been able to, I'm trying but I just can't..."

"Savannah." The way he says my name silences me immediately. "If you don't cum, I don't cum, it's as simple as that." He states plainly and presses a kiss and nuzzles my inner thigh while he stares up at me with those molten eyes of his. "Say the word and we stop. No questions asked."

I quickly shake my head, "No, I don't want to stop."

Logan smirks wickedly and my stomach flips in response. "May I resume then?" he asks gesturing to my sex with his brows, and I smile, spreading my legs a little wider for him.

"By all means," The words barely leave my mouth before his mouth is on me again and it doesn't take him long to push me back up to the apex of orgasm. My back arches off the table, my toes curl and I'm gripping the edge of the table so tight my knuckles are about to split.

"Ohh, fuck, fuck, don't stop, please Logan don't stop." I plead with a whimper while I rock my hips, rubbing my clit against his mouth desperately chasing that much sought-after release. I'm so wet that I feel my arousal dripping down to the pearl of my ass.

I don't know how he manages to do it, but somehow he pushes me through that barrier that's been holding me back and it's like a damn breaks inside of me. The built-up pressure explodes, and a lukewarm glow spreads through me, sparks of electricity in my veins causing my body to shake and convulse wildly. "Oh fuck, fuck, I'm coming. Ahh yes, yes, Logan!"

Logan groans against my pussy and the vibrations of his vocal cords travel through me and it's all I need to go soaring over the edge. My breath catches and I momentarily forget to breathe, every coherent thought, every instinct I have is quelled as surge after surge of heavenly pleasure crashes over me.

I breathlessly chant Logan's name while riding out the very last spasm of my orgasm until it ebbs away before I collapse onto the table. My limbs suddenly feel too heavy and quiver uncontrollably while I lay there bare and my body damp with sweat. *"Holy fuck,"* I pant. Logan kisses up my stomach toward my breasts, stopping to suck on my nipple. I open my eyes and look down at his gorgeous face, unable to take my eyes off him, watching keenly as he swirls his tongue over my nipple and sucks. I hiss and arch up, pushing my breast further into his hot mouth. "Mm, I've been missing out."

"Oh, you absolutely have sweetheart, that was just basic foreplay. I was giving you a little taster of what's to come." Logan states with a wayward smirk. "I'm going to fuck you so good and deep you're going to have difficulty remembering your own goddamn name," he adds, taking my nipple between his teeth and tugging it just hard enough to make me gasp against the sting.

"Uhh, Logan please..."

"Fuck, come here," Logan lifts me to a sitting position on the table and his mouth attacks mine. We kiss hot and hard for a couple of seconds until he pulls away leaving my mind in a haze. "Get down on your knees. I want to see those pretty eyes staring up at me while I fuck your throat." He growls, dragging his lips over mine as he speaks.

Logan lifts me off the table and I obediently kneel in front of him. He takes hold of my chin and tilts my head up so I'm looking up at him. I feel even smaller in comparison to him in this position, but there is something so erotic about having him standing over me all authoritative, robust muscles across his tattooed chest and shoulders, and ropes of veins down his forearms.

"You're so beautiful, Savannah." He praises. My lip's part when his thumb brushes against my mouth and I suck it when he pushes it into my mouth. *"Fuck."*

God, that sexy moan of pleasure resonates through me and I instantly crave more of it. I've never been so desperate to pleasure a man. Logan takes hold of his shaft and brushes the tip of his dick against my lips. My lips eagerly part for him and I slide out my tongue so he can rub the underside of his dick against it. "Fuck *Savannah*," he groans smearing his pre-cum all over my lips. Logan watches with hooded eyes as I lick my lips and moan. "You like the taste of me, baby?" he questions gruffly as he gathers and fists my hair. I nod slowly in response.

"Yes, I want more."

Logan licks his lips and bites down on his bottom lip, "I'm going to give you more baby, I'm going to give you more than you'll know what to do with." He vows while he slowly pushes the head of his cock into my mouth. "Fuck, that's a good girl. Let me see you open that mouth. Open wide for me. Oh, you're going to swallow my big cock like a hungry little slut. Show me what that mouth can do."

Well, this is new. Why am I suddenly okay with degradation? If I must be honest, I'm not just 'okay' with it... I'm unashamedly aroused by it if the ache and gush of liquid arousal between my legs is anything to go by.

The barbell of Logan's frenum piercing drags along my tongue as he pushes himself deeper into my mouth and his cock twitches as he stretches me. My eyes start to water when the head of his cock hits the back of my throat, but I fight the gag reflex and keep my focus on the carnal look in those deep grey eyes of his while he watches me.

"God baby girl, look at you, you look so goddamn gorgeous with my cock down your throat." He moans, gripping my hair tighter and drawing his hips back slowly and thrusting into my mouth again. "That's it baby girl, ahh fuck yes, suck it, milk my dick for every drop."

I flick my tongue against the barbell, and I'm rewarded with the deepest, sexiest moan I've ever had the pleasure of hearing. My name flows past his lips almost in a plea. "Savannah." Those gloriously thick, muscular legs tremble when I suck him harder, all the while delighted that I have the power—even if it is brief—to make him weak in the knees.

"Goddamn it, baby." Logan moans thrusting slow and deep into my mouth. "You've got my cock so fucking hard. Oh, you're going to make me cum down your throat—fuck you're going to make me cum so hard."

I'm very limited to what I can do with him fisting my hair. Logan leans over and grips the edge of the table with his free hand as he continues his assault on my mouth. We fall into a rhythm; each time he thrusts and starts to draw back I hollow my cheeks and suck him hard making him visibly tremble and curse. I've never allowed anyone to ejaculate in my mouth before. The thought alone made my stomach turn—but with Logan, I don't know what it is about him or what he's done to me, but I'm disturbingly eager to feel him explode and give me a taste of his seed.

His member starts to pulse, and his breathing hastens, "Do you want my cum baby? Ahh fuck, you're going to swallow every last drop like a greedy little slut, aren't you?" I could only moan in response, but I keep my eyes on his. I want to remember the look on his face and absorb every sound he makes when he orgasms.

"Oh fuck, ahh Christ. I'm coming for you, you ready sweetheart?" Logan pants, pushing his cock to the back of my throat. My eyes water but I can't stop watching him. I'm completely captivated by him. Logan's mouth hangs open, his cock swells and with a guttural moan he spills rope after rope of warm cum down my throat which I swallow. "Fuck, Savannah." He groans, his body jerking with every jolt of pleasure that surges through him, his cock pulses while he rocks his hips slowly, relishing the last euphoric moments of his orgasm.

It wasn't until Logan slid himself out of my mouth that I felt the dull ache in my jaw. I've been so focused on pleasuring him that I didn't even realize that the side of my face is damp where I had tears streaming while fighting off the urge to gag. Logan brushes away the tear stains with his thumb and bites his lip, staring down at me intently with hooded eyes. "You took me so well, sweetheart," he acclaims affectionately while caressing my cheek. I revel in the warm glow that spreads through me at his affirmation and find myself leaning into his touch. However, before I could even contemplate a response his hand is gone from my cheek. He reaches down to take hold of my hands and help me back up to my feet.

"Are you okay?" He asks concerned, while sweeping away strands of my hair from my face, his eyes roaming over my face. "Let me look at you. Did I hurt you?"

"No, not at all." I answer breathily. Upon hearing my response, I notice the concern he held in his gaze moments ago vanish, leaving his molten eyes glimmering with heated desire once again. "I really enjoyed it. I've never allowed anyone to come in my mouth before, but I like the way you taste." I admit bashfully, my cheeks growing hot under his intent stare.

Logan smiles errantly and tucks his finger under my chin tilting my head back slightly, so my lips are slanted across his. "I bet we taste even better together," he whispers closing the small gap between our lips. On a moan, I part my lips for him when he slides his tongue into my mouth seeking out my own.

Hands down the most erotic kiss I've ever shared with anyone. The way our tongues glide across one another's causes my brain to short circuit, especially the way he moans every time I teasingly suck on his tongue. The sweet and salty taste of us combined is simply intoxicating.

Lips still locked, Logan sweeps me up into his arms bridal style and carries me through his condo. Less than thirty seconds later, I'm thrown down onto a bed with him towering over me like an errant Sex God sent from heaven to wreak absolute havoc on not only my body, but my mind. While I lay there looking up at him, every orifice of my body is aching for this sinfully gorgeous man.

"Spread those gorgeous legs for me, baby." My legs fall open for him without reservation and he smiles, pleased. "That's a good girl," he commends, running both his hands up my thighs and squeezing while he shuffles closer and rubs the barbell of his piercing over my clit. I gasp and my hips instantly lift off the bed. "You like that? Feels so fucking good, doesn't it baby?" I bite my lip nodding and rocking my hips up, but he pulls back, and I groan in dissatisfaction. "You want more?"

"Yes."

"Beg for it." He commands tapping the head of his cock against my clit, making me shudder.

"More, please, Logan I need *more.*"

"Atta girl, you look so beautiful right now. I fucking love watching you beg for me like a cock-starved little slut," he groans, rubbing against my clit once again making me writhe and moan. "Fuck, baby, your pussy feels so good and I'm not even inside you yet." He moans hoarsely, pressing his cock against me and pulling it back slowly to admire the string of sticky arousal that stretches between our genitals. "Jesus Christ, look at that, look how wet you are for me, Savi. My cock's just gliding through your slick folds so perfectly."

"Ohh Logan, that feels so good, please don't stop." I whimper pleadingly while rocking desperately against him.

Logan leans down and presses his forehead to mine, "There's no stopping until you come for me, sweetheart. You have no idea how hard I'm fighting the urge to slip it inside you. I'm dying to feel your tight pussy stretching around me." Logan states, rubbing his shaft against my clit faster and I cry out fisting the sheets. I've never felt anything like it, the friction of the piercing against my clit is unbearable but in the best way possible. Each brush of the studs against me makes my body visibly quake. A jolt of fulgent pleasure ripples through me and I can already feel that all familiar pressure building deep in my groin.

"Kiss me, please..." I plead breathlessly and curl my fingers at his nape and pull his mouth to mine. Logan moans against my lips and we kiss feverishly while we buck against one another almost violently.

"You're driving me insane. The wetness, the taste, the smell of your pussy is making me crazy." Logan growls, biting and sucking on my bottom lip, and I whimper. "Yes baby, that's my baby, grind yourself harder, you look so good using my cock to pleasure yourself, you dirty girl," he whispers to me.

Ugh, he's so unbelievably hot.

"Oh yes, yes, ohh *Logan* I'm coming again, I'm coming..." My back arches up and every muscle in my body tenses as I soar toward my climax. Logan slows his thrusting but keeps the pressure as he takes me over the edge; I whimper and shake with absolute rapture whilst I orgasm.

Logan presses his forehead to mine and watches me fixedly all the while whispering dirty things to me as I come apart under him. "Oh fuck, yes baby, that's it, come hard for me. I can feel your clit pulsing against my dick." He groans, his lips brushing against mine as he speaks in a deep silky tone.

My hips continue to writhe against him until my orgasm ebbs away and I sink back into the mattress panting. "Fuck."

I feel Logan smile against my lips as we kiss slow and deep for a minute. He presses affectionate kisses along my face while I recover. Looking at us you wouldn't think we're two strangers that only met a couple of hours ago. The way we kiss with such fervent need and how obsessed I am with the way his body fits so perfectly with mine. We're wrapped tightly around one another, my legs coiled around his waist trapping him against me. Two orgasms in and I'm still aching for more of him. No man has ever made me feel such things and now I'm concerned I may be addicted.

The tip of Logan's member is pressed to my entrance and when I slowly rock my hips he groans gutturally into my mouth. My nails rake down his muscular back as we continue to kiss passionately. We're both completely lost in the moment and when I instinctively tighten my legs around him and buck my hips up, the smooth tip slides in. We both moan out loud.

"Fuck." Logan curses, squeezing his eyes shut as he fists the bed covers. Not the smartest move going bareback with a stranger, but in that moment of passion there was no rational thinking. I want to feel him with nothing between us. I need to feel him throb and spill his hot cum inside me. I'm not a complete idiot; I'm on the pill and I have my checks every six weeks, so on his end he has nothing to worry about. I should be freaking out but I'm oddly calm.

"Savannah," There's a tremor to his tone when he says my name. Every muscle in his back is taut and I know he's thinking the same thing I am. Trapped between doing the morally right thing and pulling out or fucking it all to hell and burying himself all the way in and risk it. "Fuck baby, wait, wait... what are we doing?" he groans nipping at my lip, his thighs are quivering where he's fighting himself for control and I find that so incredibly sexy and it only makes me want him more.

"God, I don't know, but you feel so good." I moan, rolling my hips upward drawing him in a little further. Logan hisses, his jaw clenched tight.

"Shit, so do you Savi, so fucking good. I'm burning to just bury myself in you, but we can't baby, it's far too risky." He defends, drawing himself out, but not completely and pushes back in again, his body quivering against mine. There's no denying that he wants this just as badly as I do.

"I'm on the pill and I'm clean," I whisper in his ear, and he draws back to look down at me, his eyes searching mine.

"So am I," he admits, brushing his lips over mine. "You absolutely sure you want this? It's not too late, I can pull out and get a condom."

I tighten my legs around him and nod, "I want to feel you. Every inch, every drop." All hesitation vanishes at my admittance, and he slowly buries himself all the way. "Ooohhh," I gasp and dig my nails into his shoulders when he fills me completely. My pussy stings as it stretches to accommodate the length and thickness of him.

"Baby, you feel good—you feel too fucking good. You're unbelievably tight." Logan groans and he goes still while my body adjusts to his size. He kisses me slow and deep to distract from the uncomfortable ache between my legs. We rock together unhurriedly at first, feeling one another out and when the stinging disappears completely and I'm moaning out loud, he lifts my arms and pins them above my head, he picks up the pace and he thrusts hard and deep. The sound of our moans, the creaking bed and our hips slapping together fills the room.

"Fuck, Savi, I can't get enough of you," Logan pants. Sitting up, he lifts and pushes my legs back over my head and thrusts into me hard and deep. "You feel how hard you make me, baby. Ah yes, yes, show me, show me how good you feel, scream for me while you take my big cock."

I've never been a screamer during sex, but with Logan I scream until my lungs burn, each orgasm he fucked out of me made me scream louder until my throat became hoarse. I got bent into positions I didn't even know my body was capable of getting into.

"Ahh fuck, there it is, you're clenching, you're coming for me again. Fuck, fuck, I'm so close. You're going to make me come, come with me sweetheart, come on my cock while I come in your pussy." My walls clamp around him and he growls thrusting into me from behind with short but hard strokes. My back is pressed against his chest, his hand gripping my throat, his mouth sucking and biting at my neck. "Yes baby, yes baby, just like that, squeeze the cum out of my cock, milk me fucking dry." I cry out, my body shaking violently against him while I orgasm for the fourth time. Logan follows me over, groaning and grunting my name with every burst of pleasure.

Unable to hold myself up any longer I collapse back against him, my heart hammering violently against my ribs, panting to fill my deprived lungs with much needed oxygen. Logan and I fall back onto the bed, a clammy, sticky, fucked out mess.

When he vowed that he would fuck me till I'm legless he absolutely wasn't jesting.

Though my body is aching, and I've lost my voice, I have no regrets. Logan Pierce has awakened something in me, something I have every intention to keep exploring.

Chapter 6
Logan

♡

Sweat - Zayn

Saturday morning comes all too soon, and I find myself wishing it was Friday all over again. What an unexpected night that turned out to be. When my buddy Jack all but dragged me out of the office to have a couple of drinks I assumed the night would be just that. Two guys having a couple drinks and then heading home. I had absolutely no intention to meet a woman, let alone take her to my beach front condo and spend the night fucking her like an untamed animal.

I open my eyes and blink out the bright, morning sunlight beaming into my bedroom. I'm still naked from the night before where we collapsed onto the bed, arms and legs entangled like a pretzel. She fell asleep draped across my chest. I look over at Savannah fast sleep beside me, she's laying on her front, her long blonde hair splayed on the pillow, the white bed sheet only just covering her perfect ass.

Goddamn, what a magnificent sight she is to wake up to.

No woman has ever looked so perfect in my bed before her. Images of the night before flood my mind and I groan inwardly when my dick swells and throbs in remembrance also.

47

I roll onto my side, resting my head in my hand, I admire her. Reaching up I brush a loose strand of her hair away from her pretty face. She stirs and moans softly, snuggling further into the pillow. I find myself envious of the pillow. I want her snuggling into the crook of my neck. I want to feel her warm breath against my skin when she exhales softly.

Jesus, will you listen to me? When did I become such a needy twit?

Though, I must admit I've had my share of hook ups and I couldn't wait to get them out in the morning. The state of some in the morning was most certainly disturbing to say the least. You wake up to a completely different person lying next to you in comparison to who you left with the night before. Savannah, however, is even more gorgeous in the morning than she was the night before, even with her mascara slightly smudged under her eyes, her lips still stained pink from her lipstick and swollen from a night of passionate kissing.

God help me, I want to kiss her again.

Before I could stop myself, my fingers are trailing down the length of her bare spine. I can't contain the smile when she quivers and moans quietly when I brush a kiss to her forehead. Those stunning honey-colored eyes slowly open and she blinks up at me tiredly.

"Hey you."

She smiles sleepily and sighs, "Hi."

"Sleep well?" I ask threading my fingers through her silky tresses. Savannah nods, licking her lips.

"Exceptionally well." She replies, her voice delicately hoarse from sleep and where I'd had her screaming for God hours before.

"Are you sore?" I push and her cheeks turn a rosy shade of pink.

She shrugs, her eyes briefly drop to my lips then she lifts them up to meet my gaze again. "That depends solely on what part of my body you're referring to, Mr. Pierce."

My hand travels down from the base of her spine, my fingers slowly peel the sheet off her body, and I give her ass a gentle squeeze and smile when she sighs lustfully for me. "Name every part that aches sweetheart and I'll kiss it better."

Savannah smiles impishly and bites down on her luscious lower lip, "We may be here a while if I do, however, at this moment there's only one excruciating ache that requires your exclusive attention."

I press a kiss to her bare shoulder, keeping my eyes on hers while I caress her left buttock. "Is it... this spot right here?" I whisper brushing my fingers through her damp folds and Savi rocks back against my fingers moaning softly.

"Mm yess..."

Shit. I was hard before... but just feeling the dampness of her cunt against my fingers has my cock hard as an iron rod. Last night was supposed to be a one off but who am I kidding? I need to fuck her again. I want her to ride my face until she smothers me in her tasty girl cum.

Any reservations I may have about my depraved actions in that moment got shoved into a box to deal with later, because right now all I crave is another taste of Savannah. I shift to lay on top of her, pressing open mouthed kissed to her jaw, then her neck until I'm licking and sucking down the column of her spine.

"Logan..." she gasps, stunned, fisting her pillow when I spread her ass cheeks apart and circle my tongue around the pearl of her ass. Savannah tries to squirm away, but I grip both her ass cheeks firmly and keep her in her place. "Wait... Logan wait... what are you... ohhh." She moans burying her face into the pillow when I push my tongue into her impeccably tight anus. "*Holy shit,*" she tenses immediately.

I fuck her gentle and deep with my tongue while my fingers stroke her clit with slow lazy circles. Once the surprise of my assault on her ass wears off, I feel her relax and start to enjoy the feel of my tongue gliding in and out of her tight hole. She rocks her hips back falling into rhythm with me, when I thrust, she grinds herself back impaling herself deeper with my tongue.

Goddamn, her moans are like music to my ears. I can't hear enough of it. Savannah twists and looks back at me over her shoulder when I pull her up onto her knees until she's on all fours so I could lick that perfect pussy to a slow climax. I want to savor every moment I have left with her.

I tease the tip of my tongue over her clit and smile when she lets out a low sensual groan and grinds herself back against my mouth. She's so damn receptive to my touch, I fucking love it. I work two fingers into her and rub that sweet spot buried deep again and again until I feel her clamping down on my fingers so hard that I can barely move them.

I watch with joy as she unravels for me. Her beautiful body tensing and convulsing, those whimpers of pleasure while she climaxes is enough to drive me to the edge of insanity. I give her peachy ass a firm slap and squeeze and she moans.

"Come here." I flip her onto her back and scoop her into my arms till she is straddling me. Our lips, like two magnets come together and we kiss fiercely, biting, sucking and tugging. "I have to fuck you," I groan between kisses, and she responds by coiling her legs around my waist and grinding herself against my shaft.

"Fuck me," she says impatiently and curls her fingers in my hair, drawing my mouth urgently to hers. Her heated kiss sends my already sexed up mind into a frenzy. "Take it, take what you want."

And those words done me.

With a growl I spear my dick inside her with one swift stroke and her gasp lingers in the air around us for a second. "Jesus..." I moan pressing my forehead to hers; she's even tighter in this position, she's practically choking my cock and it's taking every ounce of self-control I have not to blow my load there and then.

When the throbbing of my dick seizes, I start thrusting into her and we quickly fall into a rhythm. We fuck each other like two possessed animals that cannot get enough of one another. Her scorching mouth on my neck biting and sucking hard enough that I know she'll leave a nice mark behind— a temporary, yet pleasant memento of our impassioned rendezvous.

Savannah climaxes with an ear-piercing cry and the intensity of her orgasm sets off mine. I grip her hips firmly and she grinds herself down onto my dick, milking my cock for every last drop of come.

"Happy Birthday," I pant against her lips, and she smiles lazily.

"Thank you," she breathes, drawing her head back slightly so she could look at me properly. "It's certainly one to remember."

I smile and nuzzle my nose along her jaw. "Spend the weekend with me."

Savannah draws her head back and stares at me for a long moment. "Uhm, I can't. I have to work this evening."

I frown and continue to rub her hips. "On your birthday?"

She nods, "Yeah, I have this small event I'm overseeing for my boss while she's off at some retreat."

Retreat my fucking left nut, I bet she's off drinking herself into a stupor with her socialite friends.

Despite my current state of annoyance, I nod and draw her lips to mine. I kiss her tenderly, taking my time to savor her intoxicating taste and the way her silken lips sensually move over mine. Every deliberate stroke of our tongues and breathy moan that emits from her causes my cock to stir and swell inside her.

Savannah's eyes flutter open, she smiles impishly against my lips when I fill her cunt, "Again?" she murmurs.

"Again." I groan and shift so I can lay her on her back. My body covers her small frame, her slender arms and tanned lean legs coil around me. I draw my hips back slow and thrust into her with slow and deep strokes.

"Uhhh, Logan..."

————————

"OH, RIGHT HERE. THIS IS ME."

I glance up at the apartment building as I roll to a stop in front of a white two-story village style apartment. A well-kept, freshly trimmed lawn, three topiary shaped trees lined just under the windowsill to the right of the apartment on the ground floor. "Thank you for driving me home."

I kill the engine and shift in the driver's seat so I can face her. My eyes rake over her clad only in one of my white dress shirts that is one too many sizes too big for her petite frame. Though there is absolutely no denying that she looks agonizingly sexy especially paired with the heels she wore the night before. Fuck, I almost palm myself through the thick material of my jeans when my cock twitches zealously. Just knowing she's completely bare under that shirt is making me crazy with unbridled lust.

"You didn't really think I would allow you to jump into a taxi dressed like that, Savannah?" I point out with a smirk, and she looks down at herself and chuckles.

"Honestly, I'm eternally grateful that you didn't. I'd imagine that would have been a rather embarrassing car journey given my lack of um... under garments." She replies, smiling timidly while fishing through her black clutch for her keys to avoid looking at me while her cheeks flush crimson.

I sigh and inwardly start counting to ten to distract from the unruly situation growing in my pants. What has this girl done to me. She's got my insides burning up like a wildfire.

Lord, have mercy. I've not been this horny since I was sixteen years old, and I couldn't keep my dick down for longer than five minutes.

I smile and rub my index and middle finger along my jaw. "Well, it's the least I could do. After all, I did tear apart every single item of clothing you were wearing and as an added bonus I got to see you in one of my shirts." I express and openly allow my eyes to cascade over her bare thighs where the shirt has risen exposing her smooth upper thighs. "You're lucky this car doesn't have a back seat, or you'd already be sprawled out losing what voice you have left screaming my name while you come for the seventh time in..." I trail off and look at the time on my dash, "...thirteen hours." I finish.

A slow, shaky breath emanates from Savannah when she turns her hazel eyes to look at me, she swallows thickly and despite us staring ravenously at one another, it doesn't escape my attention that she has her thighs pressed together a little tighter.

God, I can bet my left nut that my words have that gorgeous pearl of nerves throbbing for attention and I'm bursting at the seams to dive in and deliver. "It's a true shame indeed." She sighs, her tone laced with just as much disappointment as I'm currently feeling, "I better go. I still have to get ready for work."

I nod silently, I press my molars together so tight my jaw starts to ache dully. Savannah opens the passenger side door and climbs out. With a sigh, I follow suit and walk around the car toward her and lean against the hood. "Thank you for an unforgettable birthday, Mr. Pierce." she says smiling faintly and holding out her hand to me. I look down at her outstretched hand for a beat and take it into mine. Eyes locked we stare at one another, exchanging flirtatious smiles. When her fingers enclose around mine, I tug her to me, and she lets out a gasp of surprise.

I couldn't let this be the last I see of her. I just fucking couldn't.

My hand slips away from hers and I place my hands at her hips and draw her body against mine until she's standing between my legs. Savannah watches me closely when my fingers brush away stands of her hair that blow into her face from the gentle breeze. "Thank *you* for a remarkable night, Wildfire. You've left a taste in my mouth I absolutely won't be forgetting in a rush."

Savannah licks her lips and smiles prettily while she drags the pad of her index finger along the collar of my white t-shirt. "Wildfire?" she intones, lifting her amber eyes to mine.

I nod, my lips slowly inching closer to hers. "Wildfire," I repeat and gently graze her lips with mine as I speak to her quietly. "You've got me burning up with desire like an uncontainable wildfire."

Savannah parts those sensuous lips to speak but I close the gap and swallow her words, kissing her ardently, transforming whatever she was about to say into a faint moan that has every hair on the back of my neck standing on end.

My fingers comb through her hair while we kiss and she curls her fingers at the nape of my neck, drawing my mouth even closer and deepening the kiss like the keen kitten she is.

I would love to keep devouring that sensational mouth of hers, but my lungs start to burn in protest, and we're regrettably forced to end the kiss. We stand with our foreheads pressed together, eyes closed, panting softly. "If you keep kissing me like that Wildfire, I'll be obliged to throw you back into this car, take you back to my place, tie you to my bed and spend the weekend doing unlawful things to you." I avow, my thumb caressing her jaw tenderly and she sighs, leaning into my touch.

"Well, that'll sure beat spending the evening trying to please a bunch of snooty socialite wannabes." she complains with one breath and moans with the next when I kiss down the column of her neck.

"Savi!" We jump apart when we hear a female voice screaming her name. Savannah twists in my arms and looks back at her apartment. I follow her gaze and see her friend from the night before hanging out the window grinning from ear to ear. "Han, you can call off the search party, she's home in one piece and sucking faces with the fox from last night."

Savannah groans, mortified and turns to face me, an apologetic look on her face. "And that's my cue," I rub my jaw and smile awkwardly when the girls wave at me and wave back.

"I'd like to see you again." I say, veering my gaze back to hers when both girls disappear inside.

Savannah's lips curl into a coy smile, her cheeks reddening. "You would?"

I lick my lips and nod, "As soon as possible."

"I'd like that too," we share a meaningful look and I pull her closer, slanting my lips over hers I brush a lingering kiss to her silky lips.

"Then I'll be seeing you, Wildfire." I assert, taking hold of her chin and she nods.

"I'll be waiting, Mr. Pierce." She voices flirtatiously and draws back slowly, her eyes never leaving mine. I watch her intently, my lip between my teeth until she unlocks the door and looks back at me one last time, she flashes me a sultry smile before disappearing inside.

I close my eyes and exhale slowly, desperately trying to suppress the rational voice screaming all the reasons I should walk away before I get sucked in any deeper.

Though, I've got a feeling it's too late.

Savannah has given me a taste of something I never knew I wanted, something I am now burning for.

Chapter 7
Savi

Middle of The Night - Elley Duhe

"Bitty!"

I heave an audible sigh and lean against the tiled wall of the shower while my two best friends pound incessantly on the door. "You can't hide in there forever. Get your skanky ass out here and dish the dirt!" Hannah bellows from the other side of the door.

"I'll be out in five minutes. Can I please just shower in peace!" I shout back at them laughing while I pick up the shampoo bottle and lather up my hair.

Venice and Hannah have both been hounding me since the moment I walked into the house, eager to find out what happened between Logan and me.

When I step out of the shower I stand in front of the steamed mirror and wipe my hand across it so I can see my reflection. It's odd, I don't look any different, but I definitely feel... different. My muscles ache with each movement, even more so after the shower, and my vagina feels awfully tender—which is expected after hours and hours of sex.

My eyes lower to the love bites along my neck. I brush my fingers over it and close my eyes reliving the moments Logan gave me each one. My stomach tightens and I feel giddy all over again.

After I finish my shower, I find both Hannah and Venice in my bedroom sprawled on top of my bed waiting for me. Hannah grins when I walk in and sits up animatedly. "Jeez, you were in that shower for a while. What were you trying to do in there, purify your sins, saint Savi?" Venice jokes.

I smile, flipping them both off and walk over to my closet to pick out my outfit for the event I'm overlooking this evening. "Well, I'm sorry to leave you both stewing but washing out sand took much longer than I anticipated."

"Sand?" they both repeat at the same time. "Okay, you're going to have start from the beginning, Bitty." Venice demands. "We want to hear every sordid detail."

I sigh and bite my lip, "After we left the bar we got into his Ferrari and Logan took me to his beach front condo in Solana."

 "Beachfront condo? Well, I'll be damned, not only is he absurdly hot, he's also wealthy." Hannah states shifting to lay on her front. "Nice catch, Bitty. You've caught yourself a hot sugar daddy. Now get to the sexy stuff. What's he like in bed? Does he have the goods?"

I pick out a simple black mini dress and turn to face the girls. "Girls, I'm not fazed by his wealth, he seems like a decent man. And he certainly has the goods all right, and he takes no prisoners when it comes to using it." I explain with a lustful sigh and sink to the bed. "You girls know I've never been able to climax through oral, but God his mouth and the things he could do with that tongue should be illegal. The sex I've been having before Logan was nothing like what I experienced last night with him." I turn and face the girls, "Every spot his mouth touched on my body felt like it was on fire. I couldn't get enough of him and the filthy, degrading things he kept saying to me. He had me screaming for hours and by morning I woke up to my voice like this."

Hannah and Venice listen intently while I go into detail about the things Logan, and I did to one another. "Good Lord, did it just get like outrageously hot in here?" Hannah murmurs fanning herself.

"What did I tell you, older men are so much better in the sack. Was I right or was I right?" Venice points out, hugging the stuffed animal Trent gave me when we first started dating.

I laugh and nod, "Yes, you were absolutely right as per, Vee."

"You will be seeing him again, right?" Hannah questions giving me a pointed look and I shrug.

"I mean he did say he wants to see me again... *as soon as possible,* but we didn't exchange numbers or anything, so I'm not going to hold my breath." I sigh, standing and taking off the towel to put my underwear on. The girls and I have seen one another naked on many occasions so it's become second nature stripping off in front of one another.

While I got myself ready for work, I couldn't help but wonder if I'll ever see him again.

THE EVENT WENT as I had predicted. Celeste Pierre is notoriously known as the bitch that can't be pleased. She voiced a couple of complaints but overall, she and her guests were pleased. By eleven o'clock my feet are throbbing, and I am ready to call it a night and go home.

"Savannah, the kitchen area is all clear. The catering company is asking if they're good to leave?" Kelsey, one of the waiting staff hired for the event questions.

I wince rubbing the balls of my sore feet. "Yes, you girls can go too if everything is done. I've got to wait for my uber anyway, so I'll finish off here." I tell her and she nods in understanding. "Thank the girls for everything, they did a great job as always. Get home safe."

"You too," she gives me a wave untying her apron and she turns to walk back toward the kitchen.

Fifteen minutes later the venue is cleared, save for a couple of their own workers waiting on me to wrap up and leave so they can lock up. I send photos of the night and a quick debrief to Susan before I head out.

"Thank you, Craig." I call out to the handsome owner of the venue who is stacking bottles of wine behind the bar. He smiles charmingly back at me and gives me a wink.

"Later Sav. Drop by for that drink anytime."

I nod and yawn tiredly, "I'll drop by with the girls one weekend, I promise. Keep that bottle of Chablis chilled for me."

He throws the empty box over the bar and grins. "You got it, sweet cheeks. I'll be holding you to that promise."

The company I'm interning at hires Craig's venue Blue Lagoon out frequently to hold private lavish dinners and exclusive mixers, so I've become well acquainted with Craig and his staff.

I open the door and walk out, my head down scowling at my phone trying to order an uber on the stupid app that refuses to function whenever I need it. It's been unsuccessfully searching for a driver for the past twenty minutes. "Shit," I fume and almost hurl my phone across the street.

When I look up to see if there are any taxis around I could possibly hail, I see a black and red motorbike parked right outside the venue. My heart damn near tore through my chest when I see Logan leaning against said bike, his muscular arms crossed over his chest watching me intently and looking like an absolute wet dream.

"Need a ride, Wildfire?" he drawls licking those sinful lips.

I stare at him utterly stunned, likely resembling a deer in headlights. My mind unable to invoke any words at that moment. How on earth did he know where to find me?

I only had two glasses of prosecco, so I know I'm not drunk and seeing things.

"Logan?" I utter taking a couple of steps toward him. "What are you doing here? How did you know where to find me?"

Logan smiles and straightens from his leaning position. Those molten eyes openly skim over me. "I have my ways," he replies ambiguously. I narrow my eyes and cross my arms over my chest smiling playfully

"Do you have stalker-like tendencies that I need to be made aware of, Mr. Pierce?"

Logan grins and casually walks over until he's towering over me and I'm craning my neck to peer up at him. "Not until I met you," he murmurs, grasping my chin and tilting my head back. "I'm here to kidnap you. Would you have any objections to that?"

I stare up into his eyes and my heart starts to flutter wildly in my chest. "Hmm, that will be contingent to what you plan to do with me once you kidnap me."

"Whatever I want," comes his husky response and my knees shake and almost buckle at the demand laced in that sexy deep tone. I moan when he lightly drags the tip of his tongue along my bottom lip teasingly. "You've been on my mind all day, Savannah." He rasps taking my hand he presses it to his crotch making me gasp when he grinds his rock-hard erection into my hand. "My tongue longs for your taste..." he groans, gripping my jaw with his free hand and sucks my tongue until my head goes faint. "And my dick is fucking aching to be choked by your incredibly tight cunt."

"Oh God..."

Logan swallows my whimper with a hard and bruising kiss. I was ready and willing to go off with him the moment I saw him standing there. I've never felt so needed and desired in my life by anyone and if I'm honest I'm becoming perilously addicted to the way he needs me.

That demure girl I was less than twenty-four hours ago is lost somewhere inside me. I've gotten a taste of what it feels like to be bad, and I want to be bad with him, bad *for him*.

I want him to use me in every way and any way he desires to.

I want this magnificent man to ruin me.

I want to be consumed by him and be his and his alone.

"Say yes."

"Yes." I moan a breathy response with absolutely zero hesitancy. "God yes."

Logan kisses me feverishly again until my lungs burn and I'm forced to unwillingly pull away to suck in a long greedy breath. "Come on." Logan takes my hand and pulls me toward his bike. My mouth goes dry at the mere sight of it. I've never been on a motorbike before. "Hey," I tear my startled gaze from the bike to look at Logan. "It's completely safe, I promise you."

Apprehensive, my eyes move over to the bike again and I exhale, inwardly willing my heart to stop beating like it's about to give out on me. "Do you trust me?" Logan murmurs pressing a kiss to my temple. My eyes close and I nod mutely. Oddly enough, I do trust him, which is bizarre because I don't even know him, but here I am about to climb onto his motorbike and go off with him for the second night in a row.

"Good girl."

Sweet Jesus, the way he calls me that has all my reservations melting away. Logan helps me put my helmet on and I watch him closely. Admiring his gorgeous face and the way he's biting down on his lip while he fastens the buckle securing the helmet. "Don't be afraid sweetheart, just hold on to me and remember to lean with me when we turn a corner. It may feel like we're tipping over but we're not, okay?" I nod warily and Logan smiles as he turns and gets on the bike. He looks back at me and holds out his hand to help me on. "Come on, Wildfire, jump on."

I ignore the way my stomach protests at the mere thought of sitting on the damn thing and take his hand. "You good?"

"Mhm, I'm good."

"Atta girl," Logan takes both my hands and wraps them around his waist. "Hold on tight and don't let go, understand?" he instructs, and I utter an inaudible okay. My chest is pressed against his muscular back, the spicy scent of his aftershave surrounds me, and I find it calms my nerves. Logan puts his own helmet on, and I jump out of my skin when he starts the engine and the bike roars to life.

Don't freak out, Savannah, you've got this. It's just a really fast, really dangerous bicycle.

My arms tighten around him to a point I'm sure I'm cutting off his air supply when the bike starts to move. Thankfully Logan rides slow the first couple of minutes and once the apprehension leaves my body he gradually speeds up. Okay, perhaps I was scared over nothing. It's rather exhilarating. We roll to a stop at a red light and Logan rubs his fingers affectionately over mine.

I smile frivolously, his touch triggers the butterflies deep in my belly to take flight and flutter wildly. While we wait for the light to turn green I allow my left hand to wander freely, my fingers grazing up his inner thigh, slowly inching toward his crotch. A white Mercedes AMC rolls to a stop beside us. The male driver turns to admire Logan's motorcycle. My cheeks burn when his eyes lower and he notices my hand very noticeably pressed against Logan's enlarged member.

I should have stopped, pulled my hand back, but I didn't. Instead, I find the zipper to his jeans and start to unfasten it while the driver watches. Logan does nothing to stop me, he only moves his hand from mine to caress and squeeze my bare thigh. I gasp when my fingers brush against warm flesh instead of the material of his boxers.

Holy shit, he's not wearing boxers. That's so freaking hot!

I fleetingly wonder if I should stop and behave myself, but Logan unbuttons his jeans and readjusts himself. The driver's dark eyes veer and lock with mine when I grasp Logan's engorged shaft and stroke him. He licks his lips, ravenously watching me stroke Logan steadily, who whirrs in pleasure. I feel the muscles in his back tense and the vibrations of his moans travels right through me.

The light turns green and Logan speeds off leaving our spectator behind likely palming himself. What have I become? The old me would have died of shame to pull such a risqué stunt like that, but this version of me found the entire ordeal incredibly arousing. My panties are soaked through, so much so that I'm sure my arousal has seeped onto the pillion seat.

The cool late-night breeze feels like heaven against my flushed skin. Not the smartest idea jerking off a man while he rides a motorcycle at sixty miles per hour, however the feel of his dick growing thicker and harder in my hand makes it damn near impossible to stop.

So, I don't.

I continue to stroke him, using my thumb and smearing the pre-cum that oozes from the tip over the ridge where he has his piercing which causes him to shudder. I wish I could hear him moaning, but the engine of the bike is far too loud to make anything out.

A couple of minutes later—much to my dissatisfaction the bike rolls to a stop at the front entrance of the Le Grandeur Hotel. I stare up in awe at the luxurious hotel before me. This hotel is one of the most exclusive, not to mention *costly* hotels in San Diego.

And here I sat on the back of a motorcycle with Logan's hard cock grasped in my hand. *How classy.*

My eyes flitter over to the doorman and the valet about to walk over, and sheer panic fills me. Thankfully, Logan covers himself with his helmet as the valet makes his way toward us.

I bite my lip and watch him discreetly stuff himself back into his jeans and quickly do it up before he helps me off the bike.

"You're filthy." He growls avidly in my ear once he pulls the helmet off my head and hands it to the young valet. My cheeks burn red hot, but I force myself to look up at him and hold his gaze when he lifts the hand that I used to stroke him and sucks my thumb with a low groan at the second-hand taste of himself. Holy Hercules, the insatiable look in his grey eyes has my stomach entwined into a million knots. "I taste good on you."

I swallow hard.

Could this man get any sexier?

"Welcome back, Mr. Pierce." The valet greets, rudely interrupting the moment. Logan turns to look at the Valet and smiles handing over the keys.

"Take care of my girl, Andy."

The boy nods with a courteous smile. "I always do, Mr. Pierce."

Logan hooks his arm around my waist and keeps me at his side as we walk to the entrance of the hotel several employees greet him by name. "I take it you come here often." I point out when I notice the young receptionist waves and smiles at him flirtatiously.

Logan smiles handsomely and gives me a side long stare. "I do, yes."

My insides burn as if someone just lit a fire deep inside my chest. My eyes sweep across the hotel's lavish lobby, my eyes locking with every young woman looking in our direction. Likely wondering what a refined and successful man like Logan Pierce is doing with someone like me. I mean, we're in a hotel with no luggage so I think it's patently obvious to everyone with eyes and a brain why we are here.

Exactly, how many women has he brought here before me?

Don't you even think about asking that question, Savi. He's not your boyfriend, you have no right to be jealous. It's a fling, a meaningless, casual fling.

While Logan checks us in I drop a message to the girls in our group chat that I'm with Logan, so they don't worry.

Han:

What?! Two nights in a row?! Bitty, you've got him hooked, bby!
Vee:
That's my girl! Call him Daddy, men love that!

I scrunch up my nose at the last message and type a text back.

Me:
I'll do no such thing!
Vee:
Don't be a bore, you whore! If he's a dominant lover—which he seems to be, it will drive him absolutely wild. And if he calls you a 'good girl', he's for sure into it!
Han:
I second this. Just whisper it into his ear or while you're on your knees. Look into his eyes and say, 'fuck me like I'm yours, Daddy.'
Me:
Well, he does but what if he gets put off by it? He might not be into the whole Daddy thing.
Vee:
You won't know unless you try. Stop playing it safe, Savi! That's the beauty of flings, experiment girl!

Well, she does have a point. I look up at Logan, chewing my lip contemplatively. He's having a conversation with the front desk manager.

Daddy.

Logan takes the keycard from the receptionist and turns to look at me. He catches me in a stare, watching him like a lustful adolescent. He grins, "Ready, baby girl?"

And I melt. *Fuck.*

Logan laces his fingers with mine and leads me toward the elevators across the lobby. We stand side by side staring up at the numbers at the top indicating which floor the elevator was on. I clear my throat and glance around the lobby, "Boy, if looks could kill, I'd be dead and buried ten feet under right now."

Logan looks at me quizzically. "What?"

"The deathly stares I'm getting from all your... *admirers*." I state with a chuckle and roll of my eyes. Logan laughs and the deep erotic sound of it makes me stare up at him admiration. He takes hold of my chin and leans down to brush a kiss to my eager lips.

"I wouldn't spare a thought about them, sweetheart. If I were you, I would be thinking about all the sinister things I'm going to do to you up in that suite."

My throat goes bone dry, but I keep my composure.

"Exactly how many other women have you done sinister things to up in that suite?" I probe, raising a questioning brow. Logan draws back and stares deeply into my eyes.

"You'll be the first." My eyes search his for a long moment for any signs of insincerity and that fire I had simmering in my chest slowly diminishes. "My prior visits to this hotel have been for solely business, not pleasure... until now."

I smile, satisfied by his response. That question would have singed a hole into my head had I just let it brew. I know I said I wanted to be bad, but that doesn't mean I would settle to being some man's floozy either... irrespective of how goddamn hot he is. I would hate for him to think I'm some common whore throwing herself at every and any man that moves.

The elevator pings and the doors swing open. The lift attendant smiles and gestures for us to enter. "Mr. Pierce. Miss." He greets politely and pushes the button to the forty-second floor.

Logan and I stand side by side in the elevator, our fingers brushing over one another's, we exchange heated looks while the young boy hums along to the elevator music. Logan stares at my mouth and swallows hard when I bite my lip, gazing up at him through my lashes.

Had we been alone in this elevator I know for a fact Logan would have had me pressed up against the mirrored wall, his lips attacking mine. My palms start to get clammy, and my heart picks up its pace the closer we get to the top floor.

Logan's hand wraps around mine and he draws me closer to him until our shoulders are pressed together. Our eyes interlocked, I feel that all too familiar gravitational pull, an intense invisible force drawing my mouth to his. Our eyes close, lips less than a breath apart. I part my lips for him and just as he's about to close the gap, the elevator comes to a stop.

"Penthouse suite."

Our eyes open when we hear the elevator attendant announce our floor and we pull apart. The door opens and Logan takes my hand, hands the boy a hundred-dollar bill and hurriedly pulls me out of the elevator. "Have a good night." The young boy says with a knowing smirk as the doors shut.

The white double doors to the penthouse suite to the left and it seems we are the only ones on this floor. As soon as the elevator doors closed Logan rounded on me. We came crashing together like two crazed creatures desperate to become one. Our lips, teeth and tongues clash; moans, pants and hushed murmurs filled the corridor as we stumble back toward the door.

"I underestimated you, Wildfire." Logan groans pressing me up against the door, his mouth hot on mine while he speaks to me in a low gruff tone. "That little number you pulled on the bike..."

I look up at him, dread twisting in my gut. Shit was he mad? Did I go too far? "Are you... mad?"

Logan presses his forehead to mine and smiles, "Fuck no, baby, I'm not mad. You jerking off my cock while someone watched was such a fucking turn on. In fact, it took everything in me to not pull over on the side of the road, bend you over the bike and fuck you savagely while everyone passing by watched."

"Oh," I smile against his lips. "I've not done anything like that before, but the way he was watching us made me..." I trail off with an impious sigh when he drags his lips down the length of my throat.

"Wet." Logan whispers palming my ass and squeezing. "I know, you left a delicious, sticky wet patch on the seat, you dirty girl." I vaguely hear the beep of the door's lock being activated before it's pushed open. In one motion he pushes the door and scoops my up into his arms. My arms and legs wind around him while he walks into the suite and kicks the door shut before pressing me into the door again, his mouth devouring mine with earnest.

"I brought you here to celebrate your birthday," he asserts between kisses. "I had a whole thing planned but fuck Savannah, I think I'll die if you ask me to stop right now," he admits with an anguished grunt.

"Please, don't stop." I lament, curling my fingers at his neck and dragging his lips back to mine. "There is nothing I want more than you right now."

"Christ, I want you."

"I'm yours."

And upon hearing those words, he tears open my dress...

Chapter 8
Logan

—♡—

Its All Over - Adam Skinner & Dan Skinner

GOD HELP ME, I'm a *sinner*.

No amount of repentance will ever rid me of the sins I have stowed with this young woman the past couple of days.

Why couldn't she be ten years older. Actually, if I'm wishing for stuff, I'd wish to be ten years younger so I could believe in the possibility of us being something more than a random hook up.

But I can't keep her.

She's twenty-one and I'm forty.

I have a son who is the same age as her.

My only saving grace is that she's of legal age, we're both single and our little tryst isn't hurting anyone.

I'm foolishly choosing to navigate through my instincts and completely ignore my moral compass which is screaming at me to walk away.

After tonight. I tell myself. After tonight, I'll let her be.

My mouth waters just watching her spread out naked on the bed ready for me to take her—to own her.

I move over to her, and she lifts her leg and presses her foot to my chest stopping me. When I give her questioning look she smiles wickedly up at me and leans up on her elbows. I lift her foot and press an open-mouthed kiss to the inside of her ankle. For as long as I've known myself, I've always been an avid ass and tits kind of guy. Foot fetish was never my thing, but with Savannah, her legs and feet are sensational and every time I see that fucking silver anklet and the matching toe ring on her middle toe it makes me weak.

I run my hand down her silky-smooth calf and suck her toe. She moans watching me with wide lustful eyes. "I want to watch."

"Watch what, sweetheart?"

Savannah bites her lip and pulls her foot out of my hold. "I want you to show me what you do to yourself when you think about me."

Goddamn it.

My dick is rock hard.

I grasp her jaw and stare down into those warm honey-colored eyes, "You want to watch me jerk off?" I rasp and she nods licking her lips. "Does it make your pretty pussy wet when you think about me jerking off while thinking about you?"

"Yes," she breathes sucking on my thumb when I drag it across her plump lips.

"Okay, but after it's my turn, understand?"

Savannah watches me fixedly as I back up toward the chair opposite the bed. My shirt is already discarded somewhere near the entrance where she clawed it off my body. My black jeans are already unfastened and hanging loosely on my hips. I push them down my legs, kicking them aside as I take a seat in the chair and spread my legs wider.

"Show me," she requests, keeping her impassioned gaze on mine, her bottom lip clasped between her teeth.

I spit on my cock and wrap my fingers around my shaft stroking slow and steady lubricating my shaft. I use my free hand to massage my heavy balls and caress my perineum. A ripple of pleasure slowly surges through me with every stroke. Having Savannah watch me pleasure myself has my cock hard like fucking granite. My eyes close and I stroke harder and the same time as rocking my hips up so I'm fucking my fist imagining it's her tight cunt I'm ramming my cock into.

"Ahh fuck, Savannah," I rasp, biting down on my lip. Her sex a teasing scent in the air, heavy and so addictively sweet makes me shake with utmost need for her. *Fuck*, it's almost too much, picturing all the things I'm going to do to her. I squeeze the base of my cock with one hand and tease just the head with the other, holding onto that euphoric feeling as it starts to spread from my balls, slowly making its way up my spine. Fuck, fuck, I'm going to cum, I'm going to cum so goddamn hard. Pre-cum trickles down my shaft.

I open my eyes and look at her, sitting there with those gorgeous legs spread giving me a perfect view of her cunt glistening delightfully. "Fuck Savi, do you see what you do to me, baby?" I pant, jerking my cock harder, pushing myself to the edge of sweet release, "How you make me fuck myself into a frenzy thinking about you."

"Harder, fuck yourself harder for me, Logan." She moans licking her lips rapaciously.

I abide and jerk my cock harder and faster until I feel that pressure build up deep in my groin as I reach the apex of my climax. "Ahh fuck, fuck Savi, I'm coming, I'm fucking coming for you, baby." My cock throbs and pulses and I groan out her name while jet after warm jet of cum spills coating my chest and stomach. "Savi." I pant slowly stroking out the final seconds of my orgasm until it subsides.

I open my eyes and watch her slide off the bed and fucking crawl over to me.

This girl is something else.

My cock is still semi-hard and twitching when she settles herself between my legs and takes my cock into her small hand and proceeds to lick up every drop of cum off my stomach and chest, "Christ." I growl, rocking my hips up into her hand. "Swallow my cock you insatiable little slut."

My fingers curl into her hair when she wraps her mouth around my cock and sucks hungrily working me up all over again. Within seconds I'm rock hard and ready to fuck her. I watch fixedly as my cock disappears into her mouth.

"That's a good fucking girl, you know how to suck my cock just the way I like, don't you, baby." I praise, pulling her hair away from her face so I could look into those captivating eyes.

"Yes Daddy," she moans, flicking her tongue over the barbell of my piercing. Well shit, I wasn't expecting that. I close my eyes and bite down on my lip hard, my head swims with unbridled want.

Jesus fucking Christ this girl is going to be the death of me.

"Get up." I groan hoarsely and she gazes up at me, hazel eyes all wide and needy. She obediently rises to her feet on my command. "You're making me want to do things to you I swore I would never do, Savi." I admit, gripping her jaw and staring into her eyes so she understands the gravity of my words.

"Like... like what?" she probes.

"Things that will hurt and I don't want to hurt you." I admit, brushing the backs of my fingers over her soft cheek. "I can feel my control slipping especially when you say things like that to me."

Savannah winces a little and lowers her gaze, "You're not into the daddy thing, I didn't mean..."

"Fuck, Savi no, no," I interject tilting her head up, I press my forehead to hers, "I am, you have no idea how much, but I'm afraid I'll be too rough with you."

Savannah looks up at me for a long moment, "Fuck me like you want to make me yours... *Daddy*." She affirms sultrily and I lose all my bearings.

Lord, forgive me.

"If at any point you want me to stop, I want you to tell me, and I'll stop immediately. Do you understand?" Savannah nods in understanding. "Good girl, now place your hands on my shoulders." I lean down and hook my arms under her legs and lift her till her juicy pussy is in my face.

I suck her clit and she cries out, threading her fingers tightly into my hair. "Logan..."

———

"Favorite cuisine?"

I hum mulling over her question. "I would have to say Thai, then pizza is a close second." I answer earnestly and she smiles at me warmly, sighing when I comb my fingers through her silky strands.

"Mine is pasta, anything and everything pasta." She breaks off a grape from its stem and feeds it to me. "Though lobster shack is right up there."

I chuckle and shake my head, chewing on the grape she fed me. "Lobster shack? Are you kidding me? No, you want to eat a quality lobster you go to Colt and Pistol. They serve the best lobster and burgers in the country." I clarify vehemently while picking up a strawberry from the fruit platter and feeding it to her. "They catch the lobster fresh. I'll take you next weekend. You simply must experience it. You'll never want to put another lobster or burger in your mouth again."

Savannah bites into the strawberry, her brows slowly rising to her hairline, she smiles prettily. "Wait. Are you asking me out on a date, Logan Pierce?"

I gaze into her captivating eyes, and delicately tuck a strand of her hair behind her ear. "I suppose I am, Savannah West. Do you accept my humble invitation for a date?"

Savannah laughs and nods, "When you ask me so nicely it would be rude of me to decline. Besides, you've talked this place up so much you've made me crave lobster." She sighs with a pout and rests her chin on my chest again.

After we somehow made it out onto the terrace overlooking the city, we wound up having sex on the hammock and haven't had the strength to move since.

"I can make a call to reception and see if they can have one delivered if you like?" I offer and she shakes her head.

"At two in the morning? Absolutely not, the fruit and wine will suffice." I press a kiss to her forehead when she lays her head on my chest and looks over at the city stretched out before us. "I really like it here; the view is incredible and it's so serene watching the city sleep."

I bury my nose in her hair and inhale the scent of her shampoo. It's sweet and floral, like fresh roses and cinnamon and I'm becoming exceedingly addicted to it. "Mm, it's simply breathtaking at sunrise," I murmur, pressing a kiss to her temple and I feel her shiver. I draw my head back to look down at her. "Are you cold, sweetheart?"

"No," she sighs turning to face me again. "You're actually really warm, like an electric blanket." My lips curl into a smile and my arms circle around her, cocooning her against me.

"Okay, but if you get cold—."

"I'm sure you'll find a way to keep me warm." She states with a suggestive grin and presses her soft lips to mine. I caress her jaw, and she responds with a soft moan when I push her lips apart and deepen the kiss. The hammock rocks back and forth whilst we continue to kiss methodically, savoring one another until we eventually fall asleep our arms and legs tangled like a pretzel.

I made a promise to myself that I would walk away after tonight and let her be.

It's looking like I'll be breaking that promise, because despite my best effort and intentions not to get emotionally attached, I'm really starting to like this girl.

"MM, LOGAN..."

"Mhm."

"I really should go."

I smile when Savannah practically whimpers in displeasure and curls her fingers at my nape, stopping me when I go to pull away from her lips, "Stop kissing me then." I mumble amusedly against her lips.

"God, I can't." She groans into my mouth, her tongue sneaking past my lips in search of my own. We've been parked outside her apartment for the last fifteen minutes kissing passionately like two lust-crazed adolescents. Savannah is in my lap in the driver's seat, her legs draped across the center console of my convertible. She's so petite that she fits comfortably.

We spent the entire weekend together, hauled up in that penthouse suite fucking like hypersexual rabbits that can't get enough of one another. And by God, I couldn't get enough of her. The way she's kissing me and moaning right now has me tempted to sack off work for the week and whisk her away someplace so I could have her all to myself with no interruptions, but I can't, because Monday is one of the busiest days for me at the office, especially with the Istanbul project coming up.

Fuck, I forgot all about the pesky Istanbul project. We've got the annual construction expo out there in two weeks, to which I must plan a soiree to entice the investors, so they'll loosen the purse strings and invest close to a billion dollars to build the multi-functional commerce and hotel complex.

Wait a minute, what's stopping me from asking Savi to join me? Four days away in a spectacular city with her would be an absolute dream. Perhaps I could convince her under the guise of hiring her to help me plan the get together. I'll have to check the schedule first, but I'll be sure to ask if she would consider it.

Regrettably, our fiery make out session comes to an end when my phone starts ringing, and we begrudgingly draw away, panting. I groan and utter a string of curses when I see the name on the LCD screen.

'April calling'

"Who's April?" Savannah questions stiffly, looking over at the screen when she notices the irked look on my face.

"My pain in the ass ex-wife," I answer irritably with a roll of my eyes.

"Ahh, I see," she utters with a sympathetic smile and drops a kiss to my bearded jaw. "I best get going, it's getting late, and we both have work early in the morning."

I groan and bury my face into the crook of her neck and nuzzle affectionately. "You can go but leave your lips." I state playfully and she bites her lip and chuckles. "And your pussy," I add hoarsely. "And these." I groan, cupping her perfect tits.

"Anything else?" she purrs sultrily, tilting her head back so I can suck at her throat.

"Your perfectly peachy ass, those captivating eyes, your sexy legs and beautiful feet... oh fuck it, just stay with me, because I want every goddamn inch of you."

"Keep talking to me like that and I just might be swayed." She murmurs sensually, inching those sinful lips closer to mine. I stare at her mouth avidly, my hand grips and squeezes her thigh. "Or you could come upstairs, and I can give you a tour of my bedroom." She suggests roguishly.

I moan throatily and rock my hips up, grinding my now swollen cock against her firm ass. "Such an enticing offer Wildfire, but you and I both know we will not make it to that bedroom."

Savannah grasps my jaw and slants her lips over mine, brushing them teasingly as she speaks. "My roommate will be home, so we'll have to."

I smirk, "I don't give a shit whose home baby, I'll fuck you where I want, and she can watch for all I care." Savannah's eyes grow wide, and she stares back at me taken aback. Though, the sudden spark of unruly desire and intrigue that ignites deep in her amber eyes doesn't go unnoticed by me and fuck if it doesn't add to my already raging arousal.

"I—" My phone ringing interrupts whatever she's about to say and I press my molars together to stem the mounting annoyance deep in my gut. Savannah turns to look at the LCD screen, her brows pinch together slightly and she licks her lips.

"Uhm, you should probably get that." She states slipping off my lap and back into the passenger seat. I pinch the bridge of my nose and inwardly project every curse word I could think of at my ex.

Fuck me. I divorced the insufferable bitch and yet she still somehow manages to ruin my life. I heave a sigh and take hold of Savi's hand and press a kiss to the center of her palm. "I'll call you later?"

Savannah nods and smiles prettily as she goes to reach for the door handle. "I might answer," she playfully throws over her shoulder.

"You better." I let go of her hand and take hold of the nape of her neck and draw her back to me. My lips capture hers in a slow but deep kiss that leaves us both lamenting in dissatisfaction when we pull apart. "Go, before I change my mind."

My eyes follow her fixedly as she pulls away, opens the door and gets out of the car. We watch one another the entire time she's walking around the car, right to the very moment she unlocks her door and goes inside her apartment.

The disappointment that expands across my chest feels all too real for my liking. I have never in all my life been this infatuated this quickly with a girl.

The things I'm feeling for this girl already is dizzying.

Things I've not felt in a very long time.

Things that are scaring the ever-living bejeezus out of me.

Chapter 9
Savi

Never Tear Us Apart - Bishop Briggs

"You like him!"

I groan and bury my face in the sofa cushion I'm currently clutching onto as though it's my lifeline. Hannah giggles and pokes my sides playfully while I slap her hands away laughing.

"Stop!" I protest and hit her with the fluffy pink cushion. "Of course I like him, I wouldn't have slept with him otherwise, would I genius?"

Hannah rolls her eyes good-naturedly, "No, I mean you *really* like him." She states jauntily, her dark brows rising when she stretches out the word 'really' to better elucidate her point. "And don't you dare try lie to me either. I've known you since we were in high school betch, you look at him the same way you used to look at Nathan Pratt."

I sigh remembering my high school crush. Nathan wasn't your typical arrogant high school jock. Yes, he played for the school's football team as their linebacker; yes, he was popular and so darn handsome and while those were the qualities that most of the school admired, they were not the things that attracted me to him. Nathan Pratt was kind and humble. He was smart and cared about his grades. He didn't walk around the school like he was some God unlike most of the boys on his team.

And now he's now playing in the NFL for the New York Giants. I knew he would make it, the boy was gifted and fated to go places. Yes, I do stalk his social media now and then to see what he's been up to.

He's also still so effing hot.

I sigh and toy with the corner of the cushion. "Okay fine, I do like him and honestly Han, it's daunting how quickly I'm developing feelings for him. It's only been like three days, and I don't really know much about him at all."

Hannah smiles and piles her hair up on top of her head in a messy bun. "You said he asked you out on a date, right?" she asks and I respond with a nod. "Well, clearly you're not alone in your feelings because if it was just about the sex he wouldn't have gone to so much trouble to drive all the way here to ask your friends where you were so he could surprise you."

I smile remembering the way my heart started to race at an uncontrollable rate when I saw him standing there. "I suppose you're right. God, if my parents ever found out I'm dating a forty-year-old man they would hit the roof."

Hannah laughs heartily, "Yeah, especially if they knew what said forty-year-old is doing to their sweet saintly daughter." My cheeks burn hot and I throw a cushion at her. "Ow!"

"Shut up!" I gasp mortified, yet still unable to keep the grin off my face. "I'm not a fucking saint."

"Not anymore you're not." Hannah adds with a giggle and barricades her head with her arms when I hit her with another cushion. "Ahhh, stop abusing me, you filthy little slut!"

LATER THAT EVENING I retire to my bedroom shortly after eleven. Hannah and I ordered in a pizza and binge watched The Bachelor. Venice hates reality tv shows with a passion, so Hannah and I watch it when she's at work or out with one of her 'friends'.

Usually I have a routine, I shower, do my night skincare and curl up with a book while lying in my bay window till my eyes grow heavy. That routine has now been shot to hell after the past seventy-two hours.

I turn off the lights and the LED lights around my window come on. Usually, I would close the blinds, but tonight there's a storm and I love listening to the ear-splitting roar of thunder and the rain tapping against my window. I find it really soothing, especially on nights like these when I'm feeling restless.

The book I'm reading is doing nothing to pacify the wild and errant thoughts roving around in my head. I'm an avid romance reader, have been since I was a teen. My friends don't know this, but my book choices have become more... risqué over the last couple of years. Growing up in a strict Christian household didn't give me a whole lot of freedom to 'explore' myself. I was brought up to believe that sex outside of wedlock was a great sin. Touching yourself or even having wayward thoughts was blasphemy.

My mother always told me the only man that should see you naked and touch you intimately is your husband.

While on the outside I appeared to be a dutiful daughter and abode by their beliefs and values, deep inside I've always had this licentious side to me, a part of me I kept dormant too afraid and ashamed to share with anyone. My mother drilled it in to my head that touching and pleasuring yourself was a shameful act. "God is always watching, sweet pea." She would say and that stuck with me until I was fifteen. One night, I lay awake in bed staring up at the ceiling, the house eerily quiet. My parents sound asleep in the room next to mine, my wall adjacent to their bedroom.

I couldn't sleep, there was an insufferable tingle between my legs. I've felt it before and I ignored it unit subsided, but that night I couldn't, however hard I tried the feeling wouldn't ease. I had no idea what it felt like to be aroused back then, all these feelings were new to me, but the feeling was so overpowering that I couldn't fight off the urge to touch myself.

When my fingers first brushed against my clit my body shuddered and I almost whimpered out loud but caught myself just in time and bit my lip. My fingers were instantly coated with warm and sticky arousal, my shorts soaked through.

I brushed my fingers over my clit in slow teasing circles, the tingling from before intensified and my body started to warm and get clammy. My hips rocked back and forth and bucked up into my fingers desperate for more friction and longing for more, that mind-blowing feeling slowly building deep in my groin until it consumed me.

I knew it was wrong, but in that moment, nothing felt more right. I didn't care who was watching while my body shook. I covered my mouth with my free hand to smother the cry of pleasure that crashed through me for those ten blissful seconds.

Something that is made to feel that good, shouldn't be deemed wrong or dishonorable. After that night, I couldn't get enough, it's all could think about. I couldn't wait for it to be night so I could crawl into bed and do it all over again, each night dragging it out to savor the feeling until I discovered edging and the intense pleasure that followed by denying yourself.

And that's how I feel right now. I feel that same overwhelming, burning need for Logan as I did my nightly orgasms.

The vibrating of my phone sitting beside me pulls me from my reverie. I pick it up and see Logan is calling. For a moment I stare at the phone smiling, my heart fluttering wildly in my chest. I press the green answer button and I hear his deep and husky voice in my ears through my airpods.

"Hi, Wildfire."

"Hi," I answer, leaning back into the cushions.

"What are you reading?" I go to answer but stop and stare down at the book laying open on my stomach and then turn to look at the window.

"Are you lurking outside again?" I ask sitting up and gazing out the window in search of his car, but I couldn't see clearly through the rain drops on the window.

"Perhaps." he drawls, and I can hear the grin in his voice. "I like you in red."

My eyes lower to the red booty shorts I'm wearing and bite my lip. "Why are you lurking outside my window when you could be in here tearing them off?"

A low groan reverberates through the airpod followed by a slow breath, "Because, sweetheart." He starts. "If I come up there, I'm going to do unspeakable things to you that will undoubtedly make you scream, and I would hate to put you in an uncomfortable position with your roommate and neighbors."

My lips curl and I gingerly chew on my lip, "I'm sure you can come up with a way to keep me quiet." I tease softening my tone.

"I can." His tone is tight when he speaks. "The problem there is I don't want to. When I fuck you Savannah, I want every goddamn soul in vicinity to hear you and how unbelievably arousing you sound when you come crying my name." My eyes close and I swallow thickly, my shorts dampening further. "I want them all bearing witness to how much you love being mine."

A desirous shiver passes through me, and I shudder visibly. God, there's that unrelenting, needful ache between my legs again. "Savi,"

"Yes?"

"I want to watch."

A knot forms deep in my belly, I turn my gaze to look out the window. "Watch?" I iterate and he hums on the other end of the line. "But you're not here."

"I'm watching."

"You mean right here in the window?"

"Yes, exactly as you are. Spread those legs, reach between your gorgeous thighs and play with your juicy pussy." He asserts steadily, his tone deep and laced with arousal. "Show me, I want to see how delirious with desire I make you when you're alone and thinking about me." My breathing hastens and my pussy is now throbbing with urgent need. "Show Daddy how you come for him."

"Logan, what if someone sees?"

"Let them." He retorts evenly. "You look so fucking good right now, if someone other than me is watching you, I assure you they're already beating off wishing they were filling your tight little cunt."

The rational side of me is ready to outright refuse, the thought alone of having some stranger watch me perform such an intimate and private act on myself should repel me, but that wayward voice inside of my head is intrigued. Maybe only Logan is watching, but the thought lit a fire in me that had my fingers inching toward the hem of my shorts. The rain drops on the window distorts the view somewhat and the dim color changing lights I had set to fade doesn't allow for much light.

I reach for the remote and press the red button and the color changes from warm white to red. "Fuck," Logan sighs longingly. "Look at you, baby."

My fingers slide into my shorts and glide through my slick folds until they brush against my swollen clit. I gasp; a mass of tingles travels through me. I'm so worked up and wet I know it's not going to take me long to climax. My index and middle finger are soaked, effortlessly sliding over my clit. I moan at the same time as Logan, my hips lift off the seat and rock up grinding my clit against my fingers. "That's it baby, work those fingers nice and slow over your clit for Daddy. Christ, I can hear how wet you are and it's driving me crazy."

"I'm so... so wet for you Daddy." I moan breathily.

"Oh baby, I'm so fucking hard for you." Logan responds, his voice deep and breathing heavy. "Daddy is dying to come up there and suck on that succulent pussy of yours. I want to drink up every last drop of your tasty pussy cream."

"Logan..." I whimper, pressing my fingers a little firmer and grinding myself against them harder. I faintly hear the belt buckle and zipper to Logan's pants. "Are you stroking yourself watching me?"

"Hell fucking yes."

"Stop." I order and hear him groan harshly. "No touching yourself. I want that big cock as hard as steel. I want you to be so worked up and burning for contact that the slightest breeze against your dick will make you quake."

"Savi, you're fucking killing me." He laments with a growl.

"Good," I moan sliding my fingers into my pussy. "I want you so desperate for my pussy that you're willing to kick down the door to fuck me. Uhhh, yess." I bite my lip when I feel that familiar stir coil deep in my belly. My thumb circles my clit while my fingers rub against my g-spot and I feel that pressure building and building pushing me toward the apex of climax. "Oh, I'm going to... come. Fuck, Daddy, I'm going to come so hard."

"That's a good fucking girl, you know how to please Daddy like a good little slut, don't you? Come for me baby, let me hear you."

My hips grind down against my fingers, my pussy tightens around my fingers as I soar toward the brink of release. My back arches, and my toes curl and then I come with a shuddering cry. Fireworks burst behind my eyelids. My pussy pulses and tightens around my fingers like a vise with every surge of my orgasm. "Yes," I pant, "Yes, ohh yes, Logan."

I collapse back onto the cushions, eyes closed, legs juddering while I rock against the last blissful moments of my orgasm as it slowly ebbs away leaving me a quivering mess in its wake.

"Open the door." I hear Logan growl in my ear. A very fleeting moment while I was enraptured with my pleasure, I forgot that he was there until he spoke. The line goes dead, and I force myself to sit up and get up on my feet. My legs are still shaking, but I manage to walk across my bedroom and open the door. The apartment is dark, and Hannah's door across from mine is closed and her light off which means she's asleep. Thank God, I tried to be as discreet as possible while I climaxed and while she's opposite the doors in this apartment aren't the best at blocking sound.

As I near the front door my stomach tightens with anticipation. I exhale slowly and unlock the door, opening it. The storm is still going with full force, the occasional lightening and loud rumble of rolling thunder. My jaw slackens and my eyes slowly rake over Logan standing before me dripping wet, his white t-shirt completely soaked through and clinging to his muscular torso.

He's a gorgeous sight when he's dry, but when he's wet... *Lord have mercy on my poor vagina!*

I shudder inwardly when our eyes meet. Those usually grey eyes are now almost black with lust as he advances toward me all intense and exuding such raw masculinity my knees almost buckle under his stare. I barely get to suck in a breath when his fingers curl at my throat and he draws my face to his. "Kneel," he commands lowly and my weak knees are already obeying before I could even think about responding.

My lift my gaze up to him and he strokes my jaw and lightly drags his thumb over my bottom lip. "Open." My mouth readily falls open for him. I suck his thumb when he pushes it into my mouth and his eyes close, his head lulls back and a deep guttural groan emits from deep within him.

"Fuck baby, I'm going to fucking ruin you," he hisses through clench teeth and lowers his eyes to meet mine again. The belt, button and zipper to his jeans were already undone so he pushes them down freeing his member from its confines. I stare up at it and lick my lips avidly. "I love the way you look at my cock so ravenously, like a filthy slut thirsty for Daddy's cream." He utters slowly, brushing the tip of his cock against my lips, smearing the oozing pre-cum over my lips. "Mm, I bet you would love to wear my cum on your pretty lips like lip-gloss, wouldn't you baby?"

"Yes Daddy."

"Lick those lips clean for me baby," I obey and lick my lips, moaning when the tangy taste of him explodes on my taste buds. Logan watches me with hooded eyes, his chest rising and falling steadily. "Good girl." He praises, brushing my hair away from my face. "Would you like to see how hard you made me with your little show? Do you want to feel the steeliness in your mouth?" I nod and he licks his lips. "Say it."

"I want to feel it. Let me taste you."

My lips keenly open for him and Logan slowly feeds his dick into my mouth and my God he really was hard—harder than *I've* ever felt him. The deeper he pushes himself into my mouth the louder his moans got.

I'm obsessed with the sounds he makes and I love that I'm the one responsible for each one. Every moan and breathy lustful whisper of my name urges me on until he comes close and pulls himself out of my mouth panting.

Logan pulls me up to my feet and lifts me into his arms, his mouth attacks mine with a bruising kiss. My sexed-up brain vaguely acknowledges that we are moving, but I'm so engrossed in our kiss that I only realize we are in my bedroom when the door slams shut, and I'm pressed up against it, my arms pinned above my head. Logan peels my crop top up over my breasts and while I wait for him to take it off completely, he covers my eyes with it.

"Logan... what—" The rest of my sentence is swallowed by his mouth —not that it mattered because what I was going to say leaves my mind the moment his mouth claims mine again in a dizzying kiss. I mewl and rock against the stiffness of his cock when he presses it against me.

"Whose pussy is this?" he questions, stroking the tip of his cock over my clit.

I know the answer he wants, but I'm feeling rather defiant, "Mine."

I whimper when he lands a hard slap on my left ass cheek.

"Whose pussy is this, Savi?" he repeats slow yet firmly.

"Mine. Ahh," I grit out and hiss when he spanks me again in the same spot as before. "Yours... it's yours, *only yours*." I relent and he smiles against my lips. Damn him and my low tolerance for pain.

"If you crave punishment, I'll happily comply sweetheart." He asserts pinching and rolling my nipple between his thumb and forefinger. "I'll punish you so good that next time you'll think twice before defying me."

While my tolerance for pain is almost non-existent, a part of me is intrigued. Maybe I'll take him up on that one day, but not tonight. Right now, I need him, I want his scorching mouth all over me. I want to feel him stretching me out.

"The only thing I crave right now is pressed against my pussy." I say beseechingly and part my lips waiting for a kiss when I feel the warmth of his breath against my own. Logan pushes his hand between us and pulls my shorts aside.

"Is this what you crave?" He rasps, teasing my entrance with the tip of his cock, I nod and tighten my legs around his waist silently urging him to sink into me.

"Mhm, yes,"

Logan abides and with one long stroke he fills me. I gasp, my mouth hangs open for a moment as I adjust to the feel of him filling me. The slight burn of him stretching me open still stuns me every time. Logan pulls my shirt off entirely and I lift his soaked t-shirt up and yank it off before dropping it on the floor. Our lips come crashing down on one another fiercely, kissing like our lives were dependent on it, neither of us willing to break away.

Logan's skin is damp and cool to the touch from the rain and the chill passes through me when our chests press together once he starts to thrust into me. Doesn't take him long to warm though, soon his body is hot and damp with sweat while he rams himself into me with vigor.

When he vowed before that he would ruin me, he absolutely meant it. It was three in the morning when we finally collapsed onto the bed, completely spent and unable to move a muscle. I'm still lying on top of him, chest heaving to catch my breath. My legs shaking from where he had me in the full nelson position, fucking his dick into me hard from below. I've lost count how many orgasms this man has given me the last few days, not that I'm complaining in anyway—if anything I'm making up for lost time.

I hum when Logan brushes affectionate kisses down the side of my neck, his hands roaming freely over my body while our bodies calm. "You okay?" he whispers into my ear and I nod.

"Mm, I can't feel my legs." I say with a smile, and he chuckles, moving his hands down to massage my aching thighs. "That feels nice."

"I'm sorry if I was a little too rough with you toward the end," he expresses, his tone laced with unease and I tilt my head back a little to look at him.

"Logan, you didn't push me more than I could handle." I assure him and he opens his eyes, his gaze searching mine. "I know I'm small, but I'm not some fragile China doll that will break under the slightest bit of force. Besides, what I thought I liked before definitely isn't the same as what I prefer now." I add with a reassuring smile, and he wraps his strong arms around my midriff and smiles back at me handsomely. "I've never experienced such intense passion with anyone until you. You've raised the bar quite high for every other man out there."

Logan drags his nose down the length of mine, "You're talking about other men when my dick is still buried inside you and your pussy is overflowing with my cum, Wildfire?" he rasps tightly, and I detect the tiny bite in his tone.

Okay, I have to be honest. I've never been into guys that are overly jealous and possessive, it's always been a huge put off for me, however I like the thought of Logan being envious of another man touching me. We've not discussed what this *thing* even is between us, and quite frankly, I'm terrified to even bring it up. During sex he always claims that I'm *his*, but that's just in the moment sex talk.

"You should be pleased; you've ruined all other men for me." I drawl teasingly, ghosting my mouth over his. Logan's eyes stare into mine for the longest moment, his gaze so intense my breath hitches in my throat.

"I should be, and while I can't stop you, I'm not particularly thrilled by the thought of another man touching you either." He tells me evenly, lowering his eyes to my mouth. "I want you to be mine and mine alone but going in we both knew this was going to be a short-term thing given the significant age-gap between us," he explains and drags his eyes back up to meet mine. I knew it. The knot in my stomach slowly starts to sink as the disappointment settles in. "I want to keep seeing you Savannah, I know I shouldn't, but I'm not ready to walk away from this yet."

My heart does a little flutter. I'm not ready to walk away from whatever it is either, in fact the thought of not seeing him again physically hurts. We may not have a future, but we can still enjoy what little time we do have—however long that may be.

"I'd like to keep seeing you, too." I tell him and he smiles, but it doesn't quite reach his eyes. I don't have much time to dwell on it because he closes the gap between our lips and kisses me long and deep, chasing away every thread of doubt I had screaming at the back of my mind.

We agreed to a 'no-strings' fling. We'll let it run its course and by the end of summer, which is in eight weeks we'll end it.

Sweet and casual, no expectations, no titles.

The following morning, I'm sat on a stool at the breakfast bar in our kitchen talking to Hannah and sipping on my second cup of coffee. "I had to put my earphones in because it was the only way I was getting any sleep with the two of you fucking like two jackrabbits on heat in there." Hannah gushes with a giggle and I grin into my coffee mug. "Three hours bitty, with no breaks in between, the man is a machine."

"Shhhh." I lean over and look back down the corridor to ensure the door to the bedroom is still closed. "Keep it down, I don't want him to hear you."

Hannah gapes at me wide eyed and grins, "Oh please, I spent the night listening to the man orgasm—which is hot as fuck by the way—so I'm sure he wouldn't mind overhearing my bitching about your nightlong fuckfest. I assure you Savi, that man bares no shame whatsoever about what he did to you or who overheard."

I press my lips together to smother the grin tugging at the corners of my mouth. The bedroom door opens and Logan walks out dressed in a crisp black suit and white shirt. When I see Hannah's jaw drop and she watches him awestruck, I frown before looking back and almost groan out loud.

Cheese on rice the man looks insane in a suit, so much so that I have the urge to slide off the stool, grab him by the tie and drag him back to the bedroom and beg him to do wicked things to me.

Those grey eyes lock with mine while he strides over to me, "Morning." He greets with a smile and brushes a kiss to my forehead. I swoon when his aftershave surrounds me. "I don't believe we've officially met. I'm Logan." He stretches his hand out to Hannah and she stares at it briefly before sliding hers into his.

"Hannah, it's nice to finally meet the man that's been keeping our Bitty busy." Hannah says giving me a sidelong look.

I roll my eyes at the nickname. How humiliating. Logan turns his gaze down to me, his eyes filled to the brim with amusement. "Bitty?" he questions with a smirk.

Hannah chuckles, "She hates the nickname, but we call her Bitty because she was the smallest student in our high school."

I widen my eyes and mouth the words shut up to Hannah when Logan wasn't looking, and she grins back at me toothily. "Well, the best things do come in small packages." He drawls amiably, his eyes gazing meaningfully into mine while I gaze up at him as he takes hold of my chin and brushes a chaste kiss to my lips.

"I need run sweetheart, I've got a meeting in forty-five minutes," he tells me pulling away. I nod and slip off the stool to walk him to the door. "It was nice meeting you Hannah. Oh and apologies if we kept you up last night, she may be small but she's not quiet."

I gasp slapping his shoulder and he laughs heartily. "You're one to talk," I mutter affronted, my cheeks burning beet red while I push him toward the door. Logan rounds in on me when we're out of sight and Hannah's earshot.

"You love the way I talk and I'm crazy about the way you scream for me." I moan when he hooks an arm around my waist and yanks me up against him and kisses me feverishly. We pull apart and eyes still closed he presses his forehead to mine. "Come to Istanbul with me."

My eyes flutter open and I draw my head back so I could look up at him properly. "What?"

"I'm going to Istanbul for an exhibition next week. I need to arrange a get together out there to entertain some investors. I want you to come with me as my event coordinator." He explains combing his fingers through my hair while I look up at him utterly stunned.

"To Istanbul?" I ask incredulously, he nods, and I blink up at him wordlessly, my brows furrowed. All of a sudden, my brain is incapable of forming a coherent sentence.

"Savi, I want you out there with me. My work stuff will be done in a day and then we'll have three days together. You'll love Istanbul, it's one of the best cities in the world."

I sigh, "Logan, even if I wanted to, I can't. My boss would never allow it. I'm just an intern, I'm not fully qualified to coordinate any events on my own yet."

Logan frowns, "What about the one you did Saturday night?"

"God, that was barely an event. It was an extravagant dinner party for some socialite for like fifty guests—which I had a couple of weeks to prepare for, mind you. You're asking me to plan an event for *next week* in a city I've never been to and know absolutely nothing about." I explain in a flurry and try to step away, but he takes hold of my shoulders and draws me back to him.

"Sweetheart, mine will barely be fifteen people. I can hire someone else to plan the event for me, but the whole idea is that I get to take you out there with me." Logan states, stroking his fingers along my jaw. "I saw what you did in that restaurant and that's exactly the kind of thing I'm looking for. You can do this in your sleep, I know you can."

"My boss—" I interject but he presses his finger to my lip silencing me.

"Don't worry about your boss, all you have to do is say yes and I'll take care of the rest." God, the way he's looking at me like I'm the only thing in the world makes me want to scream yes at the top of my lungs. Four days in a beautiful city alone with Logan sounds like an absolute dream come true. "Just say yes, baby," he whispers, brushing a tender kiss to my lips.

Oh, fuck it.

I close my eyes and nod, "Yes," I whisper and feel him smiling against my lips. "Just so you know, having inappropriate relations with clients is a big no no and if Suzan—my boss finds out that you and I are sleeping together she *will* have me out on my ass." I inform him solemnly and his brows knit, his eyes narrowing as though he's searching for words.

"Sweetheart, I don't want you fretting over a thing. I'm going to take care of everything, okay?" Logan affirms austerely and cups my face with his large hands. The way his eyes are gazing piercingly into my own eases the sudden bout of nerves that surfaces. "And if she does find out and decides to let you go, I'll hire you as my *personal* assistant." He jests brushing his nose over mine.

I chuckle amusedly and shake my head, "If I were to work for you, I have a feeling I'll be spending more time on my knees under your desk or on top of it than actually working at my own." Logan grins and kisses the corner of my mouth.

"Mm, perhaps it wouldn't be such a terrible thing if your boss did find out about us. I'm now picturing all the places in my office I would just love to fuck you on or up against."

I laugh softly and draw back a touch to look up at him. "You, Logan Pierce, are a wicked, wicked man." I purr sultrily and walk him back toward the door while he smiles charmingly, tightening his grip on my hips. "My legs have yet to recover from your devilry last night *and* this morning."

"So, they should that was some of my best work." He quips cheekily and buries his face into the crook of my neck. "Fuck, you make it so hard to leave you."

I sigh lasciviously and tilt my head back when he nuzzles and kisses my throat, "Then don't." I moan quietly circling my arms around his neck, my fingers splaying at his nape. "Stay and let's go back to bed." Logan groans and caresses my ass.

"That's very tempting Wildfire, but we both have work and I have that stupid thing I need to attend tonight." I pout, and he smiles, brushing a kiss to my lips. "Don't look at me like that sweetheart. I'd much rather spend the night with you, believe me." He admits, combing his fingers through my hair and pressing his forehead to mine. I notice the troubled look written all over his handsome face so I don't press further. Though I do wonder what it is he is doing tonight that's got his feathers all ruffled. "Get some rest tonight and recuperate, because you're going to need it the next time that I see you."

I smile and bite my lip, "I look forward to it."

Logan kisses me into a stupor once more before he pulls away and we walk to the door. "I'll see you Wildfire."

"Better make it soon, Mr. Pierce." I reply with an impish smile and lean my shoulder against the door after I open it to watch that absurdly fine man walking back to his car.

While I observe Logan getting into his car, I couldn't help silence the voice in my head telling me that I'm biting off more than I could chew by agreeing to go away with him. I can already feel myself getting a little too emotionally invested in this 'fling'. I just hope I don't wind up in a worse position than I was when we met—heartbroken and worthless because Logan Pierce has the potential to break me in ways I'm certain I'll never fully recover from.

Chapter 10
Savi ♡

Sam Smith - Stay with me

I GET to work a little after nine. Suzan doesn't come in until after eleven, when she's done with her daily one on one Pilates session with Jude. I set her green superfood juice in the cooler in her office so it's ready for her arrival.

While the office is still quiet and before the emails start piling in and the phone starts ringing off the hook, I fire up my computer and search up venues in Istanbul for Logan's event. I'm feeling rather giddy about the whole thing. Firstly, I've never travelled further than Los Angeles and that was for a class trip to Universal Studios.

My parents are hardworking, both been working since they were eighteen. They don't like to travel and while we weren't considered poor, they always opted for saving their money for a rainy day instead of spending it on a lavish vacation.

Traveling is my dream; it always has been since I was a little girl. Which is why, I chose to become an event planner, more specifically weddings is the route I would like to specialize in but I love all aspects of the job. Growing up I wanted to be an air stewardess, but my mother blew a casket when I brought it up and she went off into a two-hour long rant about the dangers of flying and she didn't spend four days in labor giving me life so I could risk it for a meager salary.

It didn't matter how much I tried to convince her that flying was the safest way to travel, she was having none of it, so we came to a compromise, and I settled for event planning which now that I think about it was the smarter choice for a career. As a little girl I was a fanatic of David Tutera, the celebrity wedding planner. It's going to take time and hard work, but I believe I'm on the right path and in the best place I could be to acquire the knowledge and proficiency to become a renowned event planner like him and Suzan, of course.

My phone rings, startling me from my thoughts. When I see Suzan's name flashing across my screen. I swipe my finger across the screen and lift the phone to my ear. "Good morning, Suzan."

"Savannah," she croaks on the other end, her voice strained as though she's in agony. "I'm on my way to the hospital—"

I sit upright with concern, "Oh my God, are you okay?"

Suzan sighs down the phone and snaps at whichever unfortunate person she is with. "No, I've dislocated a disc in my lower back during my Pilates session this morning and I'm in absolute agony." She huffs irritably. "I'm going to be okay, but I'll be out for a few days it seems, so I'm going to need you to hold the fort over there until I'm back." I nod in understanding and pick up my pen to take notes while she delegates tasks and appointments that she has over the next couple of days. "Oh, and I'm supposed to be overlooking a birthday event this evening for a dear friend of mine. I'm going to need you to take point on that one. I'll forward you the email with all the details."

"Sure, no problem. I'll handle it, it's quiet this week anyway so I can catch up on all our provisional bookings. Don't worry about things here, you just focus on getting better,"

Suzan heaves a sigh, "You're a star, Savannah. If you need anything—"

I shake my head and smile, waving off her comment like she could even see me. "Suzan, I'll be okay. Feel better soon." She utters a thank you and I hang up the phone and eye it for a long moment while chewing gingerly on my lip.

Oh my.

This is great.

Well, for me that is; not so great for Suzan's back.

But I've been practically begging her for more responsibility, and it seems someone up there has been listening. I mean sure it sucks that she had to get hurt for me to get the opportunity, but as the saying goes, fate does work in mysterious ways and I'm not about to slap the gift horse in the mouth when it's handed me a chance to prove to her and myself that I am more than capable of getting the job done without her micromanaging every little thing.

A little after nine the sales team come in and the phones start ringing off the hook with enquiries. I answer a couple of emails and meet with prospective clients to discuss their events in more detail. "Oh shoot, I need to dash." I say in a flurry when I see the time is almost two in the afternoon. I take a large gulp of my coffee and gather the papers splayed out on the counter before me.

Traffic permitting, I should get to the client's house for two-thirty to ensure everything is set and ready to go for the revelries.

Twenty minutes later I'm standing before a stunning, Palladian style mansion.

"Wow."

<hr>

"AND WHAT TIME are the serving staff due to arrive?" I question the caterer while we walk through the bustling kitchen. Which is magnificently designed and awashed with modern features including expansive worktops, modern hobs and an assortment of other cooking devices I'm almost certain have not even been used.

I walk through toward the open plan living room which is set with cocktail tables dressed prettily with white rose centerpieces. The house itself is so beautifully finished and furnished that you don't need much else. In the foyer a huge white rose backdrop with the words in soft pink roses, 'Happy 40th April'. I stop and admire it, snapping a couple of photos so we can add it to our portfolio and website.

The huge hallway has two rows of tall windows, letting in a huge amount of natural light. The open feel is accentuated by two-fold-back doors.

"Staff are due to arrive any moment."

I nod while typing out a quick reply to my mom asking me if I'll be joining them on the weekend for my birthday dinner.

Gosh, as if I would miss that. I'm really looking forward to sinking my teeth into my momma's delicious homemade fried chicken and waffle.

"Perfect, please brief them to circulate with the canapés and the champagne for arrival." I say and glance down at my watch. "The String quartet should arrive momentarily, please have them setup in the backyard for the dinner." He nods and utters a got it and walks off in the direction of the kitchen.

As the time nears six o' clock, the guests are due to arrive any moment, so far, I've not seen the client around, she's still up in her room getting glammed up. I've been dealing with her personal assistant Jenna. While we work, Suzan wants us to always look professional and presentable, hence why I brought a formal dress with me to change into for the party. I head over to one of the five bathrooms in the house and change into a simple red midi dress with spaghetti straps that hugs my body nicely and freshen up my make-up. I comb my fingers through my hair, ruffling up the roots for more volume before I walk out of the bathroom and make my way down the winding staircase, holding onto the guardrail for dear life so I don't slip on the shiny marble floor in my three-inch heels.

"Sav?" I go stock-still, my blood freezing over in my veins when I hear that familiar voice behind me. Please, God, let it be my mind playing games on me and not...

"Trent?" I utter a little stunned when I slowly turn to face him. Damn, I forgot how good he looks in a suit—the beautiful bastard. "What are *you* doing here?"

Trent slowly strolls over to me, his eyes openly roaming down the length of my body and back up again, he licks his lips and my stomach clinches in response. "Fulfilling family obligations. What are you doing here?"

Family obligations? What?

I blink, my brows furrowing, "Family obligations?" I voice probingly and Trent's blue eyes dart around the house and he shoves his hands into the pockets of his pants.

"Yeah, it's my mom's birthday and as much as I hate gatherings like these, she would disown me if I didn't show up to her birthday dinner." He explains coolly and smiles, inching a little closer, "Never would have imagined I would run into you here of all places. Now I'm glad I came." He adds smiling eloquently. "Funnily enough I was thinking about you the other night."

Goddamn it. Of all the places I could wind up working it's at his mother's birthday dinner, days after he dumped me for the fourth time. Of course, this would happen to me, it's just my damn luck after all. Do you know what I hate though? The way my heart pinches whenever he smiles at me. I veer my eyes from his when they linger on mine a touch too long. "You were thinking about *me*? Why Trent? Shouldn't you be 'focusing on yourself', after all that is why you broke up with me just three days ago, isn't it?"

Trent's handsome smile falls, and he sighs, his eyes narrowing as though he's searching for the right words. "Sav, I hate the way we ended things." He reaches out to touch my arm but when I back away from his touch a hurt look crosses his features fleetingly. "My intention wasn't to hurt you, babe."

I roll my eyes and scoff, "Well, it sure as shit didn't tickle when you dumped me yet again with another one of your pathetic reasons Trent, and a day before my birthday, mind you. Who does that to someone they supposedly care about?" I fire back glaring up at him irately.

Trent reaches over and takes a hold of my hand and when I try to snatch it back, he tightens his grip. "Sav, I'm going through some shit babe, I have been for a long while now, things I really didn't want to burden you with. My parents weren't exactly the pilgrim of a happy marriage, until they got divorced all I heard night after night was them screaming at one another. I didn't grow up in a loving home like you did, my parents only got married because my Dad knocked my Mom up." Trent explains and for the first time since I met him, I see sincerity in his eyes. "I'm sure they were in love and happy once, but it's hard to believe in love when all you've witnessed growing up is what it ultimately turns into." He admits and blows out a breath. "I've started seeing a therapist to get over my fear of commitment."

My chest constricts and I force myself to swallow the lump that forms in my throat. The back of my eyelids starts to prickle when I fight the urge to cry. That's the reason he kept breaking up with me, not because I'm not good enough to be with him or he finds me too boring, but because he's afraid to commit. "Trent, why didn't you just tell me that?"

Trent closes his eyes and heaves a sigh, he scratches his forehead wincing a little, "I should have, I mean, I wanted too, but I didn't want to drag you into the mess that my head has been, Sav." Trent declares, dropping his gaze to look down at his thumb brushing over my knuckles. "You've never been the problem babe, I have." I don't know why but I'm suddenly feeling more enraged than when he dumped me all those times. What the actual fuck? Why couldn't he have been straight with me and told me this instead of dumping me and leaving me to stew in self-doubt for weeks at a time?

Jesus Christ.

My lungs burn hot, I couldn't breathe and needed air urgently. I pull my hand out of his hold and shake my head. "I'm sorry but I can't do this right now," I say backing away when he takes a step toward me. "No, please, I uh, I have to work." And with that I turn and walk toward the kitchen leaving him watching my retreating back and hurry to the backyard. It's decorated with hundreds of twinkling lights, a long table set for thirty for the six-course meal, with larger centerpieces, to the ones on the tables indoors arrayed down the middle with candles.

I place my hand on my forehead, my mind reeling while I pace back and forth in the back yard. It's always the same story with him, one step forward, three steps back. "Sav." I close my eyes and place my hands on my hips, exhaling slowly to calm the annoyance simmering under my skin. "Can we please just talk?"

"Now you want to talk?" I snap irritably. "The time to talk has come and long gone, Trent. I don't understand what it is you want from me? One second you want me, the next you're distant and making excuses to break up with me. A whole damn year I waited for you to finally be ready to commit to me, but every time you made another excuse. I gave you my all Trent every time we got back together, but you couldn't even give me half of you, so I don't know what it is you're expecting." I fume and he just stares at me looking a little shell-shocked. "My friends told me you would never fully commit but every time I defended you because like an idiot I believed you genuinely cared about me and in time you'll open up and give us a chance, but you never did, and now you're suddenly ready to share your problems with me and I'm supposed to what... jump back into your arms like you didn't dump me a couple of days ago?"

Trent takes a step toward me and I retreat shaking my head, "Baby doll—"

"Don't baby doll me Trent. I'm sick as shit of you treating me like some dispensable toy you play with when you're feeling bored or lonely and then toss aside when you've had your fun."

Trent's brows knit and he shakes his head, shoving a hand through his mousy brown hair and sweeping it back when the wind blows it into his face. "Sav, I shouldn't have broken up with you. I couldn't be the boyfriend you deserved with all this shit going on in my head, but watching you walk out of that restaurant I knew I screwed up and I've been wanting to call you because I've really missed you babe." He claims slowly inching toward me, his greenish blue eyes gazing into my own, he reaches up and cups my left cheek. "Just give me another chance, please baby doll, I don't want to lose you."

I close my eyes and for the first time his touch didn't set off any flutters in my stomach, instead I have the strongest urge to recoil like his touch singed my skin.

"Trent? There you are love. What are you doing out here?" My eyes flutter open when I hear a woman's voice behind me. Trent's eyes lift and he looks at someone over my head and smiles.

"Mom, wow look at you, you look beautiful as always." Trent whistles and moves over to brush an affectionate kiss to his mother's cheek.

"Thank you love, who is your friend?" I hear his mother question and I slowly turn and face them. Wow, I always knew Trent's mother was pretty, all you had to do was look at her son to see he came from a stunner, and no exaggeration she really is a gorgeous woman. Emerald green eyes that sparkle like jewels, her hair is a lovely golden blonde swept up into a high ponytail. She's swathed in a pearl white, low cut, mermaid style dress with sequins that hug her in all the right places. She's the epitome of perfection, however, there is something about her that doesn't quite sit right with me. The icy exterior and condescending look on her face perhaps?

Oh, good grief, please don't introduce me, please don't introduce—"This is Savannah, she's—"

I quickly intercept holding out my hand to her, "The event coordinator, Suzan sends her sincerest apologies she couldn't be here this evening, she's had a bit of an accident." I explain and she smiles a little and casts a look at her son before she looks at me again and takes my hand.

"Ah yes, Jenna mentioned that Suzan suffered an unfortunate incident with her Pilates instructor this morning," I nod and lace my fingers together in front of me. "I assume you have everything under control here?" She utters narrowing her eyes at me. There's a knowing tinge to her tone and I sneak a wary look at Trent.

"Mom, Savannah and I were dating till a few days ago. You remember the girl I was telling you about the other night?" I fix Trent with a glare when his mother looks up at him and nods before casting me a disparaging look, she drops my hand. "This is her, my Sav."

My Sav? Is he kidding me? He's never called me that, not once.

I have the strongest urge to tell his mother what a schmuck her son is, but I bite my tongue and plaster the fakest smile I could muster on my face. I need to remain professional not only is she the client, she's also good friends with Suzan. If I'm not careful one bad word from her could wreck everything I worked for and I'm not about to let that happen.

"I assure you Miss Lang; everything is under control. Your guests should be arriving shortly. I should go and do one last check to ensure everything is ready for their arrival. It was lovely meeting you and happy birthday." I say and excuse myself. Trent holds my gaze when I walk past him toward the kitchen.

Damn it, running into Trent tonight has completely thrown me through a loop and I'm struggling to push my woes over him to one side and focus on my job. If I screw this up on account of him, I'll never forgive myself.

Every instinct I have is screaming at me to get the hell out of here, and the old Savannah would have, but that's not me anymore. I refuse to be anyone's doormat, despite my feelings for Trent, deep down I know he will never value me the same as I did him.

The guests start to arrive, and I linger in the shadows, keeping myself out of sight while people around mingle and sip pretentiously on their overly priced champagne and canapés while doting on April Lang like she's the quintessence of all things beauty and grace.

I roll my eyes and take a large gulp of the champagne, wincing when the bubbles burn my throat causing my eyes to water a little. Once the guests take their seats at the tables outside, I duck away into the kitchen and let the caterer do his thing. This is where I take a half hour break and rest my aching feet while they dine. I check my phone and smile when I see a message from Logan waiting for me.

Logan:
There's a gift on your bed waiting for you when you get back home x

I smile widely and place my hand on my stomach when it twists with excitement. I type him a text back grinning down at my phone.

Me:
Please God, let it be you.

I can just envision him smiling sexily while reading my message. Anxiously I chew my lip, tapping my foot on the footrest waiting for those three dots to appear on the screen and almost squeal when they pop up.

Logan:
You'll have to wait and see, sweetheart.
You're on my mind x

"Savannah!" I jump and almost drop the phone out of my hand when the caterer suddenly shouts my name. I send him a withering glare and place my hand on my racing heart.

"Yes?" I snap, scowling at him and drop my phone back in my bag.

"Sorry, didn't mean to startle you, I did call out a few times, but you were smiling pretty hard at your phone. They're about done with the meal. The speeches are next and then they'll get to the cake." Jason, the caterer explains, and I nod.

"Thank you," I slide off the stool and slide my sore feet back into the devil heels with a quiet whimper. While the service staff are getting the cake ready to be brought out, I stand by the glass door, arms crossed discreetly watching Trent stand and give a heartfelt speech to his mom.

After his speech the five-tier cake is brought out with sparklers and they all sing happy birthday to her and when she leans over to make her wish and blow out her candles, fireworks go off. I lift my eyes to look up at them, watching each soar up and explode into a flurry of gorgeous colors.

Thankfully, so far, everything is going well. The client seems to be happy; the guests all seem to be having a great time, my job here is nearly done. A couple more hours and I can head home. I'm anxious to find out what this gift is that Logan has left me.

For the next hour or so I wander around, arrange taxis to be waiting outside for when the party is over because the guests are too inebriated to drive. I sigh watching them sip their free-flowing cocktails and drunkenly dance in the backyard. "Sav," I jump when I hear Trent's voice behind me. "Dance with me?"

I roll my eyes and twist so I could look up at him. "I'm not here to dance, I'm working." I bite out and walk back inside the house with him hot on my tail.

"Sav. Sav, hey, will you please stop for a second." Trent catches my arm and pulls me to a stop.

"What?" I hiss, pulling my arm out of his hold I scowl at him. "What do you want, Trent?"

Trent licks his lips and inches toward me, "I want you, babe." He affirms, taking hold of my hand and lifting it to his lips. "I made a mistake, I miss you Sav. I miss being your boyfriend. I miss the way you used to look at me." He inches closer into my space, eyes locked on mine until they slowly drop to my lips. "I miss tasting your lips."

My gut twists and not at all in the excited, giddy kind of way it should, no, this fucking hurt. I place my hand on his chest stopping him from coming closer and push him back. "Trent, stop." Trent's eyes lift to mine and his brows furrow. I've seen this side to him one too many times, his eyes are unfocussed, and the sour stench of alcohol on his breath makes my stomach turn. "You're drunk and on the trawl for a quick fuck, but you're not getting that from me, not this time."

Trent shakes his head, his eyes looking over my face. "Wow, since when does the angelic Savannah West curse? I've not heard you utter a single profanity since I met you." He states with a grin and places his hands at my hips and draws me closer. "Mm, I like it, why would you ever keep this sexy and feisty Savannah under lock and key."

"She's always been there, Trent, but I was always a little too focused on trying to be the perfect girlfriend for you and the honorable, obedient daughter to my parents that I completely disregarded what mattered most—and that's what *I* wanted. But you were right, you're not mentally ready to be someone's boyfriend and I'm no longer interested in being your girlfriend." I state calmly, taking hold of his wrists to pry them off my waist when the sound of the front door slamming shut echoes around us followed by slow footsteps.

Trent and I look over at the person that emerged from the door and is now standing less than fifteen paces away, both of us with different expressions on our faces. Trent's being of exasperation and mine... complete and utter bewilderment.

I stand stock still, staring unblinking into the familiar pair of grey eyes of the man I've spent the best three days of my life with. Logan stands before us, hands fisted by his sides, brows pinched together and a dour look on his handsome face that sent an icy chill down the length of my spine.

"Dad." Trent slurs and I tear my eyes from Logan's to look up at Trent.

Dad? Did he just call Logan... Dad?

Everything around me slows drastically, including my heart rate when I turn to look at Logan again and his eyes slowly lower to Trent's—his *son's*— hands intimately resting at my waist and my fingers curled around his wrists.

Oh my God.

For the past four days... I've been fucking my ex-boyfriend's dad.

Chapter 11
Logan

♡

My All - Larissa Lambert

"Yes, Suzan, I am fully aware that she's just an intern, but I've heard nothing but great things from the clients that she's worked with thus far, I mean, the testimonials on your website and all over your social media are all commending her. I'm confident that she will pull together something spectacular for this event." I tell her and lean back in my leather chair, rubbing my fingers across my jaw, making a mental note to have my beard trimmed.

"Logan, yes Savannah is great with the clients and overlooking the smaller events but she's still very new, she doesn't have the experience and connections that I do. Listen, I'll be good as rain in a couple of days, and I'll be more than happy to fly to Istanbul with you. I have a handful of contacts out there that owe me favors, I will put together such an event that by the time the party is over they'll be handing over the checkbooks to you laughing." Suzan states lowering her tone to one more sensuous in a bid to try and convince me to take her with me instead.

God, the woman is a cunning snake. Despite her being good friends with my ex, one week after we split, I ran into her at an event and since

109

then she's been shamelessly flirting and angling to get me to go on a date.

It took me nineteen years to finally be free of one shrew, I'm not about to make that mistake again, I couldn't give a steaming pile of fuck how hot she is. The mere thought alone makes my balls want to shrivel and jump back up into my body.

I stand up and walk around my office, stopping to stare out of the window overlooking the city. "Suzan, If I'm honest, I would hate to waste your expertise on something so... minimal. I'd much rather you *personally* focus on my company's anniversary gala which is next week. That is my priority, and it is far more important than some inconsequential dinner for twenty odd investors which let's be frank will be a waste of time for someone like you."

Suzan hums on the other end, "You may be right, it could be a stretch for me to take out four days right before your company's gala and you did pay the premium to have me personally organize it, though I would have given you a significant discount with benefits if you'd just agree to a dinner date with me."

I roll my eyes and pinch the bridge of my nose. There she goes again. This coming from the same woman that forbids her employees from having relations with clients.

"I'm not dating and not looking to date anytime soon. I also don't date my ex-wives friends." I assert hardening my tone, so she knows I'm not just playing hard to get. "I'll be in touch to arrange a meeting with Miss West to go over all details and arrangements. I hope you feel better soon." I hang up the phone before she could even utter a bye and release a slow agitated breath.

That woman irks me.

I WRAP up work earlier and head out to get a haircut and my beard trimmed before April's birthday bash tonight. I agreed to swing by after the dinner, I intend to spend as little time as possible with those hollow twerps she loves to associate herself with. And the one and only reason I agreed is for my son. Growing up the poor kid had to suffer watching us at one another's throats, the constant arguments, the frosty atmosphere in the house, should not be the environment a child is brought up in. I can honestly count on one hand the happy moments we shared together which was when he was a baby.

I'm not saying I'm perfect, I've surely made my mistakes throwing myself into work, never being around to avoid seeing April. My resentment for my wife and absence wound up severing the bond I had with my son and that's on me.

On my way to April's party, I stop off to drop a package to Savi. Hannah takes the black box with the satin red ribbon and smiles, quirking a brow when I instruct her to leave it on Savannah's bed.

Like a child heading to their favorite toy store, I'm excited and looking forward to the Istanbul trip with her. Having her all to myself for four days, my dick rejoices in my pants just thinking of all the wicked things I'm going to do to her.

I pull up outside the condo April has hired to throw her party and hand the key to my Range Rover to the valet and make my way over to the entrance. The door is left ajar, so I push it and walk in. I can hear voices the moment I step in and follow it until I find who the voices belong to. I see my son Trent and some woman having a disagreement. I almost turn and walk away until I catch a glimpse of the girl's face.

No, it fucking can't be.

My feet suddenly turn to lead and despite my best effort they refuse to move an inch. "Dad." I distantly hear Trent say, and my suspicions are confirmed when she turns and those amber eyes that captivate me interlock with mine and I feel heat rise up my neck, especially when I lower my gaze and see my son's hands gripping her waist, the same waist I was gripping this morning as I was ramming my cock into her. My hands fist by my sides. What the fuck is she doing with my boy? How do they know each other?

Savannah's wide eyes dart back and forth from Trent to me, a look of terror on her pretty face.

The silence drags between us and it felt like forever until I finally found my voice and forced myself to say something. "Everything all right?" I ask and cast a look at Savannah.

Trent looks at Savi and she peers up at him when he pulls her to his side and wraps his arm around her waist. My insides clinch tight and every drop of breath I had in my lungs vanishes. "Yeah, everything is fine Dad, Sav and I were just talking." Trent slurs drunkenly.

"Sav?" I intone and he nods and gestures to me.

He sways on his feet and smiles lazily, "Yeah, uh, Sav, this is my dad, Logan. Dad this is Savannah, the girl I've been dating." I consider myself a calm man, but this is one moment I'm really struggling to keep my composure. I have this burning urge to walk over to them, rip Savannah out of my son's hold and demand to know what the fuck is going on. Savannah was supposed to be working an event tonight, what is she doing here? How the hell did I wind up fucking my son's girlfriend for fuck's sake?

"Dated." Savannah finally speaks up and breaks out of his hold, likely gauging the formidable looks I've been throwing her way. "We broke up," she grits and casts me a fleeting look while I glare back at her furiously. Thank God Trent is too inebriated to pick up on the tension between us.

Savannah mentioned the night we met about her ex-boyfriend that dumped her a couple of days before her birthday, I just never would have imagined it would turn out to be my son.

This is un-*fucking*-believable, of all the women I could have met and fucked why did it have to be *her*. My stomach rolls and I shake my head, I'm too angry to talk and I can't just fucking storm off without it raising suspicion.

Fuck!

"Mom is out back, Dad," Trent says indirectly dismissing me so I could leave them alone to continue their 'talk'.

Without another word I nod and turn to walk toward the backyard. I'll wish April a happy birthday, show my face and get the hell out of here. As I walk away, I can feel Savannah's gaze penetrating my back, and it takes every ounce of my willpower to not put my fist through a wall.

This is going to do wonders for my relationship with Trent if he finds out. What am I supposed to say to him? Oh, sorry son, I've been unwittingly fucking your ex-girlfriend the past few days.

Shit, shit, shit.

What kind of perverse bullshit have I gone and gotten myself involved in.

I need to talk to Savannah and get to the bottom of this before I lose my mind.

THE NEXT HOUR or so I spend making small talk with people I couldn't stand, not that I was even listening to a word that was coming from their mouths. I'm disengaged from everyone around me, my mind is whirring and I'm still feeling irritated. My eyes scan the area in search of Savi; apparently she's working the event covering for Suzan, so she wasn't lying— that's something at least. We're both just victims of circumstance. Our twisted fates playing a very sick game on us both.

While I'm pretending to listen to Steve go on and on about bit coin investment, I catch a glimpse of Savi in the kitchen. I hate that she looks so good in that red dress and despite my annoyance I can't stop picturing myself tearing it off her perfect body.

Trent is engrossed in conversation with his cousins and April is talking with her sisters. This is my chance to slip away unnoticed and catch

Savi before she leaves. There is no way I'll make it through the night without talking to her. Jesus, I couldn't listen to Steve any longer, so I excuse myself mid-conversation and walk off in the direction of the kitchen. I loosen the tie around my neck while I look around for her. I round the corner and see her heading up the stairs.

Glancing back I make sure no one is around and follow her up the stairs, taking them two at a time. Savi's completely oblivious of my presence until I reach the top and grasp her arm, startling her; she gapes when I drag her toward the array of doors down the corridor.

"Logan, what are you doing?" she asks in a flurry looking back to make sure no one is around to see us.

At that moment, I couldn't give a toss who saw us. I open the door at the far end of the corridor which happened to be a study, and stuff her in the room, close the door and press her into it.

We stare at one another for a long moment, both our chests rising and falling hastily with every jagged breath we took. My jaw is clenched so tight it aches and throbs unpleasantly. "Is he the ex you were telling me about the other night?" I demand hotly and she peers up at me, "Say something, Savannah." I hiss impatiently and place my hands on either side of her head, caging her in.

Savi's brows fuse and she blinks up at me, "Yes, we broke up the night before you and I met."

I bite the inside of my cheek and force myself to hold her gaze and not look at that inviting mouth of hers. "Jesus Christ, Savannah, please tell me you didn't fucking know because I don't think I can stomach the alternate scenario right now."

"No, of course I didn't know." She sputters, her gaze stormy. "What the hell do you take me for? You think I planned to screw my ex-boyfriend's dad just to get back at him for dumping me? Are you being serious right now?" She retorts, her tone wounded. "You neglected to mention that you even had a kid. Besides, if he's your son why doesn't Trent carry your last name? Why does he go by Lane?"

"Because he chose to take his mother's maiden name after we divorced. We don't exactly have a doting father son relationship—no thanks to his shrew of a mother." I utter bitterly with a shake of my head.

"So, I've heard." Savannah replies with a sigh.

"Are you back together with him?" I ask before I could stop myself and Savi stares up at me blankly for a beat before she shakes her head slowly.

"No, I am not back together with him, and I have no intention to be either. No offence Logan, but your son is an egocentric prick that can't seem to figure out what he wants and I'm tired of waiting around for him to pull his finger out and grow up." Well, she's not wrong there. I've had many conversations and arguments with him about his future, but it seems to go in one ear and straight out the other.

I'd honestly get more out of a brick wall than I do him sometimes and it's so unbelievably infuriating. Trent loves the easy life his mother and I provide for him, he has absolutely no aspirations whatsoever.

He doesn't have the drive or ambition I did at his age. Life is just one big party for him and the lack of affection he got from myself I try to make up for with materialistic things—which I know is so wrong, but you need to build a foundation somewhere.

I'm not going to lie it did madden me that he mistreated Savi and hurt her multiple times and a part of me is secretly pleased she's realized she deserves better than him. Because she does, a girl like her doesn't come around often and needs to be cherished.

"So, what now?" Savi sighs chewing on her lip tentatively and I can't fight off the urge any longer. I lower my gaze to her mouth and press my molars together.

"We can no longer see each other. Even if you are broken up, you're still my son's ex-girlfriend and I can't knowingly betray him like that.

It would be morally wrong to keep seeing you." I force myself to say and Savannah nods meekly.

"No, I completely agree." She replies softly, her eyes lifting to mine. We stare at one another and the longer I stand close to her, the scent of her sweet perfume surrounding me, the harder I'm fighting the urge to close the gap and devour that mouth of hers. It's absolute torture, I'm in physical pain. "It would be wrong," she adds with a breathy whisper.

"Very wrong," I respond in the same manner. My fingers itch to reach up and brush against her soft cheek just to hear her moan for me like she does.

Hell, Logan, stop staring at her mouth you moron. What are you doing? Get the fuck out of there!

"I should probably go." Savannah says but makes no move to actually leave and I nod mutely, my arms still caging her in with absolutely no intention to move so she could go.

"I spoke to your boss earlier this afternoon, she's agreed to let you organize the get together in Istanbul." A surprised look flashes across her beautiful face. "However, considering the circumstance I don't know how appropriate it would be to take my son's ex-girl-friend on a trip with me." My stomach sinks just uttering those words and the disappointment that settles in her eyes makes me ache deeply.

"Oh, well you should take one of the other girls or Suzan, I'm sure she would be thrilled to go with you." There's a little bite laced in her voice when she speaks and had I not been royally pissed off I would have thoroughly reveled in the fact she's a little bitter about me going with another woman.

"I don't want them Savannah, I want you."

"Logan, you just said it wouldn't be right for us to go together."

I frown, mulling over every option in my head while I look over her face. There is no other option, I want her and nobody else. "Do you still want to go with me? The last thing I want is for this to raise questions because I was adamant that I want you as the coordinator." I say and Savannah nods. "Then we'll figure it out. It's a business trip, nothing more and after we get back, we cut all ties and walk away. Trent won't ever find out what happened between us and if the two of you end up working things out—"

Savannah sighs exasperated, "There is nothing to work out. I have no interest in being with him and had you not walked in when you did, I would have told him that I'm seeing someone else." She admits tilting her head up at little lessening the spaces between our lips.

"So, you no longer have any feelings for him?" I ask raspingly and she gazes up at me through her lashes. "Answer me."

"I...I don't know." She replies quietly and I wince against the sudden heaviness that settles in my chest, slowly pushing out the air from my lungs. I got to pull away, but Savannah curls her slender fingers in the lapels of my suit jacket, stopping me. "But...he's not the one I'm thinking about right now,"

My eyes veer to hers and we stare intently at one another for a drawn out moment. "No?"

Savannah shakes her head and rakes her teeth over her bottom lip. "No, I think you know very well who I've got on my mind right now." I swallow thickly.

"Christ, stop, stop saying things like that to me, Savi. You're not making this any easier for us." I close my eyes briefly and suck in a slow breath to kerb the urge to dive in a kiss her, "Fucking hell, this isn't how I had planned to end the night." I admit opening my eyes to look at her again. "Right about now I should have had you spread out on your bed, sucking on your juicy cunt while I fuck you with my fingers dragging one slow orgasm out of you at a time." Savannah's breathing goes shallow, and her eyes slide shut, a soft moan secretes past through soft lips that my cock readily responds too.

The magnetic pull is damn near impossible to resist and so are her lips. The minuscule space between us gets smaller as our lips inch closer together.

I'm a loathsome man.

And an even worse father.

TO BE CONTINUED...

Thank You For Reading

Dear Reader,

Thank you so much for taking the time to read my book. I truly hope you loved Savannah and Logan.

Don't worry, this is not the last you'll see of them. They'll be back with more sizzling and juicy adventures very soon.

If you enjoyed the book, I would really appreciate it if you could drop a review. Feedback is always welcome, good or bad.

If you're new to my books, I have many more spicy novels you can get immersed in, be sure to check them out!

About the Author

Shayla Hart is an emerging author of steamy, contemporary romance novels. This is Shayla's eighth book with many more lined up for 2023!

When Shayla is not hauled up in her writing cave, she's working full time as an events executive/wedding coordinator. Along side a full time job and writing career Shayla is also a social media creator.

She resides in the UK with her husband of seventeen years and two teenage sons.

Be sure to follow her socials to take part in her monthly giveaways and keep up with her upcoming projects.

Also by Shayla Hart

The Accidental Wife

Love Me Again

Hook, Line, Professor - Part I

Hook, Line, Professor - Part II

Hook, Line, Infinity - Part III

An Assassins Oath

Cuffed By Love

When Love & Hate Collide - Coming Soon

When Love & Fate Collide - Coming Soon

Made in the USA
Las Vegas, NV
08 September 2022

54859429R00077